D1532086

Badman's Pass

Center Point
Large Print

**This Large Print Book carries the
Seal of Approval of N.A.V.H.**

Badman's Pass

R. W. STONE

CENTER POINT LARGE PRINT
THORNDIKE, MAINE

This Circle Ⓥ Western is published by
Center Point Large Print in the year 2016 in
co-operation with Golden West Literary Agency.

Copyright © 2016 by R. W. Stone.

All rights reserved.

First Edition
July 2016

Printed in the United States of America
on permanent paper.
Set in 16-point Times New Roman type.

ISBN: 978-1-68324-044-0

Library of Congress Cataloging-in-Publication Data

Names: Stone, R. W., author.
Title: Badman's pass : a Circle V western / R. W. Stone.
Description: First edition. | Thorndike, Maine : Center Point Large Print, 2016.
Identifiers: LCCN 2016017861 | ISBN 9781683240440
    (hardcover : alk. paper)
Subjects: LCSH: Large type books. | GSAFD: Western stories.
Classification: LCC PS3619.T67 B33 2016 | DDC 813/.6—dc23
LC record available at https://lccn.loc.gov/2016017861

Dedicated to my grandfathers:
David Stone and Jacob Kotz

I've never known finer men

A brave man doesn't admit courage,
A coward don't admit fear.

—Old Western saying

Prologue

"Vengeance is mine," sayeth the Lord. Well that may be so, I don't rightly know for sure, but I suspect the Lord doesn't have to handle human frailties like sorrow, anger, grief, hate, and depression. When folks are dealing with such mighty emotions, they need a powerful motivator just to keep going, and as much as I hate to admit it, there's none better that I know of than a good old-fashioned desire for revenge.

They also say that the ends don't justify the means. Well, fancy philosophers might have a field day with that one, but if I've learned anything in life, it's that when the means are fair and the end is righteous, then how or why something plays out is fine with me. As far as I'm concerned what it boils down to is abundantly clear. Namely, you have to do whatever it takes to win as long as you're sure of why you're in the game.

I do know one thing for sure. When the Devil finally confronts the Lord, he won't care a hoot about rules or justifying the means. Evil doesn't have any sympathy whatsoever. Evil doesn't care about feelings, truthfulness, innocence, or playing by the rules. There are no rules where evil is concerned.

When they say—"All's fair in love and war."—

what they really should be adding is: "And all bets are off once the other side refuses to play fair. Anything goes." Those on the Lord's side better learn the most important rule there is—in the end righteousness won't mean a damned thing if we're all dead and have let evil win out.

Chapter One

The riders came out of the early morning mist at a full gallop, aiming straight toward the Arapaho encampment. The majority of the tribe's men were away hunting and they had left behind their women, children, and the elderly. Those remaining in the small camp were taken completely by surprise. Some were simply preparing their morning meals while others were still asleep in their teepees.

One of the village elders looked up and noticed that a few of the riders seemed to be wearing uniforms of some sort. He was puzzled because they did not appear to be exactly the same type that had been worn by the U.S. Cavalry officers who a short time ago had granted them permission to settle this area. It made sense to Gray Knife, however, that since the various Indian tribes dressed differently, the White Eyes would, too.

From the way the men were riding and the expressions on their faces Gray Knife sensed hostility. He assumed that these men had not have been told that his people had a right to be here so he tried to set things straight.

Quickly grabbing the flag that his chief had received during the treaty ceremony, Gray Knife ran out, waving it by its long pole. His people had been told by the Long Knives that it was the symbol of their trust. He did not speak much English so as he waved the flag, he shouted out the one important word he had been taught: "Peace."

It all happened so fast Gray Knife didn't even have time to react to the bullet that hit him in the chest because a sword slash took him by the throat almost simultaneously. He actually stood headless for a moment before his body toppled over backward.

From that point on it was hard to distinguish between the screams of the helpless Indian victims, the gleeful shouts emanating from the attackers, and the loud, continuous gunfire.

In some nearby bushes a small red-headed boy remained hidden. He was crouched and paralyzed with fear. The child had risen early that morning in order to surprise his mother by fetching water to start the coffee brewing. At the time, at least from the boy's point of view, it had seemed a very important task.

The boy's mother was a widowed Quaker and had taken it upon herself to spread her gospel to the Indians. That calling had taken the two of them from their home in northern Illinois all the way to the Western territory where, after six months of perseverance, stubbornness, and her never-ending insistence, she had finally been accepted by the tribe. The Indians had learned to trust and respect her devotion. She in turn had learned to love and respect the members of a tribe that simply referred to themselves as "The People."

For the next hour or so hell had, indeed, appeared on earth. The few young braves present who were able to fight were quickly over-whelmed and butchered. Horrified, the red-headed boy realized it wasn't going to end with just the men. Women were being shot, stabbed, and clubbed to death as well. No distinction was made between young, old, mothers, or women who were pregnant. Children were stomped to death under horses' hoofs. The screams seemed never to stop and blood was spilled in every direction.

Shortly after the attack began and among all the loud commotion one woman walked fearlessly through the center of the carnage and sternly addressed a small group of men who seemed to be in command. She was petite and attractive and appeared to be in her early thirties. The woman wore a clean white shirt with a large silver broach pinned to it and held a Bible clutched tightly to her chest. She, too, was red-headed.

"These people mean no one any harm what-soever!" she shouted angrily. "Stop this instant! They are here by permission of our government. You have no right to do this. Stop I say!"

A tall, heavy-set man with a dark black beard looked long and hard at her, and then turned to the man on his left. "No right the lady insists," he said, laughing. "Clay, what say I teach this Injun lover here what's right and what ain't?"

"Be my guest," the other replied, shrugging.

The black-bearded man suddenly spurred his horse forward, reached down to scoop the young woman up, and rode off into a small nearby wooded area with her. The last time the boy saw his mother she was kicking and screaming in a desperate attempt to fight off her attacker.

The child stifled a cry and bit down on his lip so hard he drew blood. His eyes remained glued to the spot in the woods where the man had dragged his mother. He remained hidden in that small bush, the whole time praying silently for help.

To the boy the wait seemed an eternity, but eventually the man with the black beard came out of the woods. Alone. He rode back to the side of the apparent leader of the group. They were now close enough to the bushes for the boy to over-hear their conversation.

"So, Brick, you teach her right from wrong?" the leader asked. He was slightly taller than the other man, clean-shaven, and wore a flat-brimmed hat with a calfskin headband.

Even through the bushes the red-headed boy was close enough to notice the fresh scratch marks on Black Beard's face and a small cut on his lower lip.

The big man sneered and nodded. He wiped his cheek with a dirty bandanna he had taken out of his pocket. "Well, I'll tell you, Clay, she was a mite reluctant to learn at first, but I stuck with it until I finally convinced her. She got my point. Know what I mean?"

The leader grinned. "So, I assume she won't be giving us any more problems?"

Brick shook his head. "Not now, not ever." He held up his hand and opened it to reveal a large silver broach. Smiling, he pinned it to his left chest as if it were a medal or trophy of some sort.

That simple gesture was all the boy could take. His fear was now gone, replaced with a type of anger he had never known before. His life didn't matter, pain didn't matter, size or age didn't matter. The boy was on fire with a burning desire to kill.

"Aaayyyeee!" he screamed as he launched himself at the bearded man. There was a large rock between the bush he was hiding in and the two riders' horses. When he emerged from the bush, he leaped onto the rock and suddenly propelled himself over the closest horse's rump and onto the big man's back.

A human child has one weapon that is almost as powerful as an adult—his bite—and the boy took full advantage of his primitive instincts. Wrapping his arms around the man known to him only as Brick, he clamped his teeth down hard on the left side of his enemy's neck and hung on for dear life.

Shots resounded all around him and screams seemed to be heard everywhere, but the yells coming from the bearded man were the only sounds that interested the boy. The more the man screamed, the more the lad bit down. While grabbing onto his foe, the boy's left hand somehow found the silver broach, and when he was finally thrown from the big man's back, the broach tore away in his grip.

After he landed on his back, the boy sat up and proudly spit out a large chunk of red-stained flesh from his mouth. Looking up from the ground, he saw the man holding the side of his neck that was now almost completely covered in blood. The boy angrily tried to stand when the man called Brick reached for a belt axe with his bloody left hand. The tomahawk was a nasty two-sided affair with a blade on one end and a hammer on the other.

"The kid bites deep," the taller man known as Clay commented with a smirk. "That's gonna leave a scar, Brick."

It was the last thing the boy heard as the hammer smashed down on his head.

Chapter Two

No one starts out saying: "Someday when I grow up I want to be a bounty hunter." I sure as hell didn't, but I do remember the day it all started.

It all began about six months after the War Between the States ended. I was traveling West, headed for a small valley I had found some years prior. I intended to build up a ranch there even though the Army hadn't left me with enough cash to buy a steak, let alone a herd of cattle.

On the way I stopped in a small town just long enough for a decent meal and to rest my tired bones in a real bed. As I recollect, for some reason or another the town was called Brannigan's Mill. Truthfully I don't remember ever even seeing a grist-stone let alone a mill.

It was about 2:00 in the afternoon and I had just stepped out of the hotel where I had enjoyed a more than passable lunch. Hot chicken potpie has always been one of my favorites, and when accompanied by a pecan pie dessert, no man I know of would ever dream of complaining about it.

I was standing on the sidewalk, right in front of the hotel, lighting up a brand new 10¢ store-bought cigar when I suddenly heard shots from down the street. I looked up and was startled to find two men in the process of firing their pistols directly into the bank. Their horses had been tethered out front of the bank, and they were mounting up when a young man ran out with a Henry rifle in his hands. I assumed he was a bank teller.

The young man from the bank proceeded to shoot one of the robbers right out of the saddle, but unfortunately the other one returned fire and killed the teller on the spot with a bullet to his forehead.

The outlaw was too far away for me to hit with a sidearm and my rifle was in its saddle scabbard. Of course, as luck would have it my saddle was still back in the livery across town where I'd stabled my horse. Helpless as I was all I could do was attempt to get as good a look as I could at the robber.

I tried to remember such details as the brown leather vest with conchos the robber wore, the gray fedora hat on his head, and the big bay horse he rode away on. Unfortunately I couldn't pick up on much else. Since I was a kid, I've always had poor long-distance vision. Things always seem to get a little blurry after a few yards.

I felt at the time that all I'd really be able to do to help out was to report the robber's description to the local authorities. Going after that outlaw was the town sheriff's job, not mine. It's not that I'm particularly selfish, mind you, but I had just finished almost four years of fighting a war for everyone else's interest but mine. This wasn't my town, I had no money in the bank, and the robber hadn't even thrown a shot my way. I wasn't planning on getting involved. To be frank, I was worn out and just wanted to be on my way.

Then, just as the robber was reaching the end of the street, a woman ran across his path, dragging her young child behind her. She was simply trying to get herself and her little boy out of harm's way. To my horror the outlaw rode right over the boy, trampling the child with his horse.

There weren't many others in the street at the time but it was immediately obvious to all of us that the boy was dead. He had been run over by a horse and its rider at a full gallop. No way he had survived. The mother held her hands to her mouth as if to scream, and then fainted.

The sheriff quickly rode out after the robber but returned alone after only three hours. "I'll need supplies and a posse equipped for the long haul to catch this one. I'm asking for volunteers," he said hurriedly. I had no choice. Not after what I'd seen. Later that afternoon about twelve of us rode out after the bank robber.

The outlaw had taken a fairly straight path out of town, but after a half hour or so had hooked left and headed for the foothills. Because the sheriff had been unable to catch him and had returned to town, the robber had a good twelve-hour head start.

That time of year darkness fell quickly so we ended up camping sooner that we would have liked.

Among those men in the posse were two or three older men who fancied themselves trail wise. After about three hours or so of sharing chow and coffee, I began to suspect that much of what they claimed to know was bluff and bluster. Since I was still unknown to them and relatively young, they all assumed that meant I was inexperienced.

I kept my opinions to myself, remembering the old saying that a fish dies because it opens its mouth once too often. In the cavalry one of my sergeant's favorite sayings was: "It's better to remain silent and be thought a fool than to open your mouth and prove it."

As long as we seemed to be on the right course, I would ride along and I really didn't give a hoot in hell what the posse thought about my opinions. As far as I was concerned, it was all of little importance when compared to catching that man.

I could tell that the sheriff, a rather stout fellow named Hans Wagner, was town bred and raised, and had very little savvy when it came to the trail. As I recall, he seemed trustworthy enough and I had no reason to doubt his bravery. After all, he had been first in the saddle and had quickly ridden out after the outlaw without any hesitation.

While it was true that none of us in that posse could say for sure what really happened during his initial pursuit or why he had suddenly turned back, I was willing, as I'm fairly sure the rest were, to give him the benefit of the doubt. He was their sheriff, they had elected him, and then, as I came to learn, reëlected him. They knew the man far better than I did, and they trusted him.

We rose early the next morning and were almost immediately back in the saddle. I was somewhat familiar with this area, having ridden it quite a few times before the war. As we rode on, I tried to pick up any patterns to the fugitive's escape route. By that time in my life I'd learned that most men when spooked ride in a straight line. A few others, however, are cleverer than that and use evasive tactics such as those I'd been taught in the war.

As long as the robber's trail was obvious, the posse seemed to have no problems following the sheriff's lead. There were no complaints until the third day, at which point the robber had cut to the south for a while, and then backtracked. The two men who held themselves out to be the posse's experts on tracking were fooled at least twice, and that cost us a full day.

The same thing happened on day five, and that's when the griping started. "I have a family I have to get back to," or "I never thought when I signed on for this that it'd take so long," were just a couple examples of the sort of complaints the men in the posse began to throw out.

The sheriff tried to keep the group together as best as he could, first by pointing out his authority, then by appealing to the group's civic obligations, and finally by using threats and other forms of cajoling.

On the sixth day I'd had enough of the ineptitude. If I'd learned one thing in the war, it was not only to think like your enemy, but to try to stay one step ahead of him in your planning. When we came to a rather wide stream and the group prepared to cross, I finally spoke up.

"Mind if I say something, Sheriff?" I asked.

The group had stopped to water the horses and to fill canteens. "Sure, what is it?" he replied.

"I don't think he went straight across here," I explained.

"No? Why not?"

"Well, I've been noticing how this fellow rides. He usually heads south for a while but inevitably he returns to a northern track. Twice he's doubled back the same way," I said.

"And you think he's doing it again?" he asked.

I nodded.

"Afraid I'll have to disagree with you, son. You see, these tracks go right across the stream here and our men have already found new ones on the other side. He's obviously going straight across," the lawman responded.

Another man from the posse spoke up: "Sheriff, I'm sure we'll have him by day's end, but not if we don't get goin' now."

I shook my head. "Looks that way sure enough, but I think this galoot is riding toward a specific destination, and that's north, not south," I explained. "He may very well have ridden across here, but he just as easily could have backed his horse up over his own tracks into the water and then ridden downstream in order to cross over farther on down."

"Hans," the other man said calling over to the sheriff, "I don't know this young feller from Adam's house cat, but you've known me for years. Lou and I already rode up and down this here stream, and we didn't find no tracks coming out."

"You didn't ride far enough," I argued. "Either that or he brushed his trail after coming out."

The man, one of the locals called Whip for some reason or another, pulled his horse along-side of mine. "That's so?" he said angrily. His intent was clear. Whip was trying to win his point by intimidating me.

"Like you said, you don't know me," I pointed out. "So don't assume you can bully me into following a cold trail." I dropped my hand to my sidearm.

The sheriff looked at the two of us. "No need for that. Remember, we're all in this together." He looked at me. "Sorry, son, but he's right. I know Whip very well, but I don't know you at all. Best we go with his advice and follow his lead. We'll continue on following the man's trail, like Whip says."

I shook my head slowly and pushed up the brim of my hat. "Sorry, Sheriff, but I didn't join this hunt for you or Whip. It's all about a boy, lying cold back in town. I gotta go my own way from here on in."

"Suit yourself, son," the sheriff said after a moment's consideration. "And good luck to you, boy."

"Good luck to you, too. But for the future, Sheriff . . . I ain't a boy and I sure as hell ain't your son."

When they rode out across the stream, I heard one of the men mutter: "And good riddance you young know-it-all whippersnapper."

Once the posse disappeared across the stream, I patted my horse on the neck and spoke to him: "Either I'm right or I'm a complete fool, and likely as not we'll end up dead. Well, I will at any rate." As I tightened up the reins, I added: "We're in for it now, but then we both know it won't be the first time." The Appaloosa snorted as if to agree with me and I gently kicked him into a lope.

Chapter Three

To the north of my position there was a small forest and just beyond that was a rather mountainous area. Either one would provide equally good cover for a man escaping on horseback. By now I was sure that was where the outlaw was headed. Once he made it deep into that terrain no posse on earth would ever find him.

It didn't make sense for me to ride down the stream desperately looking for signs of the outlaw's exit. The odds were against my getting lucky enough to pick up his track on the riverbank. Even if I did, I would still end up merely following behind him at a distance.

If my thinking was correct, I could head him off quicker by cutting diagonally across country than I ever could by riding slowly up and down a running stream looking for hoof prints or broken twigs. If I was obviously wrong, I wouldn't find him, but maybe the rest of the posse would. I didn't think I was wrong, though. Not this time.

I rode hard for two days, purposely taking the steeper climbs or the less-traveled trails. At one point I stopped to give the horse a rest and to survey my surroundings. I couldn't help thinking that under other circumstances this would be fine country to explore or perhaps to hunt in.

Constantly dismounting to walk up steep rocky hills or getting soaked fording cold streams wasn't my idea of fun. I was dead tired by the end of the third day, so at sunset I stopped to make camp.

If my reckoning was even fair to middling, I had only three more days to catch this man, whoever he was. After that the country would swallow him up and I'd never find him. As I said, all I had to go on was a quick glimpse of a bay horse, his general body size, and a fancy vest with conchos. All he'd have to do to disappear would be to change clothes and trade horses. If he did that, I'd never be able to find him.

I unsaddled my horse, replaced his bridle with his hackamore, and picketed him to the ground. While the Appaloosa was grazing, I lit a cigar, one of the many bad habits I'd picked up in the Army, and surveyed the horizon. I watched the smoke drift upward and noticed how the wind blew it down and to the left. Down and to the left. That got me thinking. I had planned to continue riding straight ahead in the morning, but while studying the hills off in the distance I made a snap decision.

By this point in time I had followed enough of his trail to know approximately where he was going. I knew that at this rate there was a good possibility I might not be able to catch him. Riding straight ahead would help me follow his sign better, but I asked myself what good would that do if it meant he would still get away?

I considered following that curve I'd seen on the horizon by riding across and down, using a short cut to the northeast, and then cutting back again. After all, the ultimate goal was the man, not the Canadian border. I finally went with my gut feeling and came to the same conclusion that gamblers are so fond of saying: "Sometimes you just have to let the dice fall as they may."

Two days later found me at the top of a hill, looking down into a small cañon. I always carried a good telescope with me, a habit I'd picked up when I first joined the cavalry. I bought this one from a sailor back in 1861. I suspect the Navy may not have actually authorized a "legitimate transfer" to the sailor, but then again finder's keepers has always worked for me and the price was right.

I took the telescope from my saddlebag and searched the valley. To say I was anxious would be an understatement. I remembered that young mother's plaintiff wails and her plea to me in town once I ran over and helped revive her: "Please help me." Of course, I realized she was referring to her child, but there was nothing anyone could do to help him. I felt the only way I could help this poor women was to bring the boy's killer to justice.

I rode out of town before I learned of the woman's religious convictions or if she even cared whether the man lived or died. All I felt at the time was a burning desire to do something for her and the memory of her boy. Catching this bastard was the only thing I knew to do.

After about two or three minutes I spotted something moving at the far entrance to the valley. It was a horse and rider. I noticed something causing reflections apparently from his belly.

"Silver conchos," I thought. I must have actually said it out loud because after I'd been quiet for so long my horse suddenly tossed his head up.

I'd been right; it was the robber. Technically, since that boy back in town had been killed during the bank robbery, he was now also a murderer. While I'll admit to feeling a sense of accomplishment, it was quickly replaced with a sense of dread. I knew that once the outlaw made it out of that valley, I'd lose him for good. The problem now was that I was on horseback at the top of a very steep hill while the robber was riding below on level ground. Once he spotted me, he'd take off in a rush for the far and yonder.

I looked down and remembered reading about that Greek horse, Pegasus, that supposedly had wings and could fly. *Damn,* I thought, *I sure wish he were here now.* If I tried going down that hill, my horse and I would probably end up flying, too. In all likelihood, however, we'd be flying head over heels.

Chapter Four

My troop in the war had a motto: "We'd ride to hell and back." It seemed as though now was the time to put that to the test. Time to put up or shut up, as they say. While I watched the rider entering that valley, I calculated my odds. They were slim to none. I replaced the telescope in my saddlebags and glanced down. Actually it was more like looking straight down. I couldn't dismount and climb down, that would take far too much time. Trying to take that hill on horseback was suicide, and I didn't have a rifle that could hit a rider galloping at that distance. *Too bad,* I thought. *I ought to have a sniper rifle with a damned telescopic sight on it.* Since that wasn't the kind of rifle I owned, it all seemed hopeless. I thought of the broken body of that boy back in town and shook my head. *No way you get away. Not while I'm still breathing.*

I dismounted and pulled the saddle from my horse and dropped it on the ground. "Sorry about this but I've got no choice," I said to the horse. "Don't let me down on this." I don't really know if I said it more to him or to myself. Years ago I had seen a Cheyenne Indian take a hill like this one and I remembered how he had managed the feat. At the time I thought he was crazy. Now it was my turn to try and I can assure you I must have been equally as crazy.

I quickly pulled my rifle from the saddle scabbard and lengthened its sling. At the time I was carrying a Spencer cavalry carbine. I hoisted it up over my neck and across my back. I next tied the reins together up over the horse's neck, went to his rear and grabbed hold of his tail, tightly. I wrapped the tail around my left wrist and slapped him on the rump with my other hand.

Now anyone who knows anything about horses will tell you it was highly probable that gelding would have kicked the crap out of me and run away instead of going down that incline. That didn't happen. Not with this horse.

I have always favored the Appaloosa breed and this one was bred true by one of the smartest Indian tribes around when it comes to horses. As far as I can tell the Nez Percé Indians of the Northwest were the only tribe to breed their livestock selectively. They valued disposition and intelligence first in their horses. My experience has been that Appaloosas are quiet and sensible with a willingness to learn I've not seen in other kinds of horses.

As a breed the Appaloosa is known for its distinctive coat color. Some call them squaw spots, but basically the horses have a solid or roan color up front and a large blanket of white and spots over the rump. Others of the breed are white with spots all over the body. The one I was riding was a blue roan with white and black spots.

Regardless of the horse's color pattern the breed seems to be very adaptable, and their endurance and speed are legendary. The Nez Percé supposedly bred them specifically to have durable hoofs and strong legs. The one I was riding was a large gelding with broad knees and strong large tendons. He had never failed me in all the time I'd owned him and he didn't hesitate now. We went down that hill with me running as fast as I could, just to keep up.

I remember trying to lean back as I ran so as not to fall forward head over heels. I also attempted to pull back on the tail in order to give the horse more balance. I don't know if that made any sense or whether or not it helped, but I do know it was better to dwell on that than it would have been to scream in terror all the way down.

I didn't die, but only the Lord knows why not. It certainly wasn't good living that did it. At any rate when that Appaloosa hit the valley floor on the run, he thankfully just stopped. It took me a full minute or two just to catch my breath. When I finally recovered and looked up, I could see that rider heading at full gallop straight toward the valley's exit.

I swung up onto the horse's back, unslung the Spencer carbine from around my neck, grabbed the reins in my left hand, and put a spur to him.

The Appaloosa started running as if he were born to it.

At that point we were heading at an angle north and west toward the end of the valley. It was obviously going to be a race to the finish and the stakes were life itself. By now the other man had seen me but was making no effort to stop or surrender. Quite the contrary, even as he rode I could see him pulling a rifle from its scabbard. I leaned forward to encourage the big gelding onward. I heard a shot and swear I felt something fly by my face so I put my head down alongside the horse's neck.

By now I was considering changing his name to Pegasus, since for all intents and purposes we practically *were* flying. The Appaloosa beat the other horse to the far end of the valley with time to spare. I dismounted and grabbed the horse's leg from underneath and brought him down to the ground. I lay down behind him with my body holding down the neck reins. I lay my carbine across the horse's side and sighted it in.

I have to hand it to that fellow. Outlaw or not he sure could ride. He was actually standing in the stirrups and firing what appeared to be a long, lever-action rifle at me. It was probably a Winchester. I hoped our low profile on the ground would keep my horse safer while giving me a better platform to shoot from.

I didn't want my Appaloosa injured but my right

hand has always been weak and it trembles some from time to time. As if that isn't bad enough, my long-distance eyesight stinks. I needed that carbine as steady as I could make it and didn't have much time to do anything else. I cocked the Spencer and set my sights on the outlaw, charging at me.

Another shot took off my hat. *Damn that bastard!* I thought. He could certainly shoot as well as he could ride. I fired back, and although the outlaw seemed to bend forward for a moment, it didn't stop him. The man rose back up again while I chambered another round.

The Spencer carbine I was using was a magazine-fed, lever-operated rifle chambered for a .56-56 cartridge that was a rimfire. The Spencer had a tube that held seven rounds, but the hammer had to be cocked for each shot. I found it to be a very reliable firearm but carbines aren't very good for long-distance shooting, especially in the arms of someone who can't see well.

I fired twice more without effect and all I received for my efforts was a bullet graze across my left shoulder. I had to wait for him to get closer into my carbine's most effective range.

I took a long deep breath, let half of it out, and squeezed off a round. The outlaw rolled back-ward and fell off his horse. I put my head down for a moment, and then stood up. The man was no longer moving.

After my horse got up, I stopped to check him over. I found a spot of blood on his side, but closer examination revealed it had come from my wound. He was uninjured and, trust me, no one could have been more pleased than I was. I remounted and rode over to the robber. When I examined him, he was dead with a bullet clear through his chest, right over his heart. If he ever had one, that is.

I remounted and rode after the outlaw's horse. When we finally caught up with it, I noticed it was a fairly decent stallion that seemed to have some Morgan blood in it. I grabbed its reins and rode back to the body. After some effort I hoisted the corpse sideways over the Morgan's saddle and tied it down with some rope that I wrapped around his legs, through the stirrups, and back up over his neck. By that point I didn't have to worry about his comfort, a fact that didn't bother me in the least.

Eventually I rode around and back up the high ridge and recovered my saddle. After washing down my wound with some water from the canteen and pouring a little whiskey over it from a small bottle I carried for medicinal purposes, I re-saddled my Appaloosa. I looked back one more time into the valley and then headed back to town.

The trip took almost a full week, and, believe me, being on the trail all that time with two horses and a dead body began to vex me. After the second day I gave serious thought to dumping the body and returning with just his saddlebags and the money from the bank. Something inside of me however told me to bring him all the way back. To this day I don't know why.

It's not that I would have felt particularly guilty about leaving his body out there alone instead of burying him in Boot Hill. Of that much I'm sure. The man had robbed a bank, trampled an innocent kid, and had shot at me. As far as I was concerned, he could rot in hell. No, it wasn't guilt. I think the main reason I brought him back was to give the woman and the town the satisfaction of seeing his lifeless corpse.

At the end of my journey I was greeted by an empty town. I didn't actually expect a crowd waving flags or someone waiting to pat me on the back and overflowing with congratulations, but here it was just the opposite. There was nothing. I realized it was still early in the morning, so I assumed everyone was either sleeping or in the kitchen having their first cup of coffee of the day. I looked down the main street and decided to tie the horses up in front of the sheriff's office. There was no joy in what I had done, but maybe I'd get some satisfaction in seeing that condescending lawman and his arrogant posse members shamed.

When I dismounted and had tied the two horses to the hitching post, I looked around for some place to eat. I was hungry and thirsty. There hadn't been enough supplies in the pair of saddlebags I carried for all that time on the trail, so I had to get along on quarter rations and the occasional prairie chicken I had managed to shoot. Right then and there I gave serious thought to finding a good pack mule for future use.

I walked across the street to the hotel and ordered breakfast. While sipping the best cup of hot java I'd had in as long as I could remember, I was approached by two men. One was wearing a black suit and the other had on a white shirt with a smooth black vest and a string tie. The one in the vest stared at me for a moment as if considering something.

"Can I help you with something, mister?" I asked abruptly. I've never been particularly sociable this early in the morning. I was tired, dirty, and was just beginning to relax. I was in no mood for anything other than breakfast.

"My name is Hobbs. I'm the mayor here," he explained. "Might I ask your name?"

"Just call me Badger. It's quicker," I answered.

"Did you just ride into town?" the man with the suit asked.

"And if I did?" I snapped back.

"Well, to be frank we noticed the body on the horse tied up outside the sheriff's office and wondered if you had anything to do with that," he replied.

"Well, you're obviously not the sheriff, so are you just asking out of curiosity?"

They looked at each other before the other man replied. "No, you misunderstand. Let me introduce myself, also," the man with the suit said calmly. "I'm Herman Franklin, the bank manager. It was my son who was killed by a robber recently. I believe you are one of the men who rode out with the posse, and since they have yet to return, we were wondering . . . is that the man who killed my boy?"

My whole attitude suddenly changed. I rose quickly and stuck out my hand to shake his. "I'm sorry for being rude. Yes, sir, he is. I separated from the rest of the posse some time back and went my own way. I caught up with the robber about a week ago. He's the one. No doubt about it." I reached under the table and brought out a set of saddlebags. "The money from the bank is in these bags," I said. I handed them over to Mr. Franklin. "It's all there," I added.

Mayor Hobbs was elated. "My boy, that's outstanding. I am personally going to see to it you get anything you want during your stay here."

I looked down at my plate. "Breakfast would be nice."

Mayor Hobbs laughed. "Of course. That one is on me personally. Least I can do. Enjoy. And after you relax and freshen up to your satisfaction, come and look for me. Meanwhile I'll take care of the arrangements for the body. You can find me over at the sheriff's office later."

"And I will of course arrange for your reward," the banker added.

"Sorry again about your son," I said. I couldn't think of anything else to say.

"Thank you," he said sadly. "He was worth more than all the money the bank ever had."

As it turned out, the robber was also wanted elsewhere for shooting a bartender and robbing an express station. There were outstanding rewards from those incidents as well. By the time I was ready to leave town I had more money in my pocket than I'd made during all my time in the Army.

Before leaving, I offered my condolences to the boy's mother. It was a very uncomfortable experience. I tried to sound hopeful and offered a few platitudes that I'd heard used far too often during the war, but I recognized the signs of depression. They were beginning to call this sort of thing shock. The woman was hardly responsive and after a short visit to her home I left. Hell, fled would be a much more accurate term. I'm sorry to say I have never been at ease under such circumstances.

I was tightening the cinch on my Appaloosa, preparing to ride out when Mayor Hobbs approached. "Sorry to see you go, lad," he said sincerely. "Stick around. Next election we might even convince you to run for sheriff." He laughed.

"I'm not much for town living," I said, shaking my head. I patted my pocket. "With this I can get a start on a ranch I've been planning for four years."

"Well, the town's eternally grateful," the mayor explained. "Anything we can do in the future, just ask."

"There is one more thing," I said.

"Just name it, Badger."

"The bank robber's horse? Any claims on it?" I asked.

"No family to claim him as far as I know," Mayor Hobbs replied. "You want him, he's yours. Just take him. No one will say a word about it, I promise you. Spoils of war, so to speak."

"Nothing quite like that," I replied. "It's just that he's a nice strong stallion and gets along well with my gelding. I want him to have a good home and I was thinking he might help me start a herd on that ranch I was telling you about."

The mayor nodded. "Good luck with that. We wish you well. By the way, mind if I ask you one last thing?"

"Shoot away."

"I was just wondering. Why do they call you Badger?"

I chuckled and swung up into the saddle. "Let's just say, if I don't get my way, I can be a real pest about it."

The mayor laughed. "Wouldn't surprise me a

bit, but in your case you'd be hard-pressed to get folks around here to consider that a negative."

"They obviously don't know me well enough," I replied. "*Adiós*, Mayor."

I retrieved the Morgan stallion from the town's livery, and then rode out with one more addition. With some of my reward money I'd purchased a large black jack mule and loaded a pack on him with extra supplies. As I left town, I never even glanced back. I'd always felt better out on the trail and was anxious to get back to my valley.

About a mile out of town I passed a large group of men riding back into town. They were dirty, dusty, and seemed all played out. It was the posse. As we passed each other, they looked over at me, puzzled. Not a word was exchanged. I merely tipped my hat and rode on. I was, however, smiling deeply.

Chapter Five

Most Western towns of the day were hardly what an Easterner would call glamorous, but this one, recently renamed Cooper's Crossing after the only successful miner in the whole area, was downright miserable. The main street, if you could call it such, was full of mud, horse droppings, refuse, and anything else that humans used for waste. On top of being an eyesore, the place stank to high heaven, and if that wasn't enough, the day I rode in there was a cold drizzle blowing that seeped into your clothing and chilled you right down to the bone. Unusual for that time of year.

By that point in time the war had been over for many years but I was still riding an Appaloosa gelding. This one was gray and black with the usual white spotted blanket pattern over its rump. I now trailed another big pack mule and on this particular day had a chestnut mare walking behind the jack and tied to the back of its pack saddle. My jacket collar was turned up and my old fedora was pulled down low over my face. Even so, I felt like someone had dropped an icicle down my shirt. Off to my right a mud-covered mutt followed me. He looked like something the cat dragged in, and for Lobo that's saying a lot.

Lobo was a dog-wolf mix, weighed about a buck twenty-five, and with everyone but me had the disposition of a plains buffalo on a bad day. I'd found him as a stray pup about four years back and raised him on canned goat's milk till he was able to fend for himself. Usually that's just what he did when I was out of sight. Then sooner or later, no matter where I was, he'd eventually show up, acting like the return of the prodigal son. That was fine with me. Out on the trail I enjoyed his company, such as it was, and there's no denying his phenomenal sense of smell had come in handy on more than one occasion.

I rode on down the street looking for the sheriff's office. I was anxious to rid myself of the load I was carrying tied crosswise over that chestnut mare and experience had taught me that the quickest place for that sort of transaction was the office of the local law enforcement officer. Off to the right about ten buildings away was the sign I was looking for. I nudged the Appaloosa over and came to a stop at a hitching rail staked out in front of the jail.

"Stay, Lobo," I said, cautioning my shaggy canine traveling companion. "None of your shenanigans while we're here in town. Got it?" Lobo looked up at me with a sort of perpetual half smile, and then walked up onto the sidewalk planking and curled up near the railing. Sometimes I doubted he ever understood a word I said.

I pulled a Springfield Model 1873 Trapdoor .45-70 rifle from my saddle scabbard, stepped up onto the walk, opened the door to the sheriff's office, and took a quick look around. Over the years I'd been in hundreds of such offices and couldn't help but notice that they varied very little. This one, like so many others, had a large L-shaped desk against the right wall and just in back of it in the far corner was a small round potbellied stove. As expected there was an old, beat-up coffee pot on it.

If experience counted for anything, my guess

was that the sheriff's coffee pot held the only decent brew in this whole town. Off to the left side of the room was a wall rack that held a half dozen rifles. I caught a glimpse of a couple of Winchester '73s, two shotguns, and some Burnside carbines. Below the rack was a series of wooden pegs from which hung a belt with a double holster and a brace of Remington single-action revolvers.

In the back of the room, directly facing the front door, was a passageway that led to the cells in back. I'd been here before and knew there were four such jail cells. The passageway was open at the time, but it could be closed up tight with a large swinging metal door complete with a locking dead bolt.

Sitting behind the desk was Jake Finley, the town sheriff. More accurately he was leaning backward with his arms behind his head and his feet up on the desk. Jake was probably in his mid-thirties, although it was hard to tell precisely because he had a large set of whiskered side-burns that covered much of his face. He was about average height but with a set of wide shoulders and, as I well remember, he had a very strong grip.

"Keep doing that and your spurs will scratch up that desk," I remarked, slapping the rain from my coat and pants. "Taxpayers might not like the misuse of public property."

The sheriff lifted his bare boots up and nodded

his head in the direction of the gun rack where a closer examination revealed a pair of spurs lying on the shelf that was directly under the rifles. "You know the rules in here," he answered dryly. "You're supposed to put the gear up before coming in."

I shrugged. "I told you before, I have to come in first before I can hang it up."

"Whatever," he replied, shaking his head. "Just take the rig off and hang it up."

I set the rifle in the corner and removed my rig as the sheriff had put it. I now wore a wide black belt with a series of cartridge loops of different sizes. Some were sized to hold .45-70 shells while a few others were larger and fit 12-gauge shotgun shells or slugs.

The belt had a rather substantial buckle, and hanging low on the right side was a large holster. Actually it was more of a sewn up leather boot top that was cut from an old cavalry officer's riding outfit. Resting in its holster was a drastically cut down side-by-side double-barreled 12-gauge express gun. After removing the belt, I re-buckled it and hung it on one of the wall pegs. When I turned around, the sheriff lowered his arms from behind his head.

Surprisingly his right hand held what is known as a Shopkeeper's Peacemaker. Essentially it was a Colt Single-Action Army Model 1873 with its barrel shaved down to about two and a half inches and with its ejector rod and housing removed. Lately they had been making them to hold a variety of shell sizes but the sheriff's retained the original .45 long Colt caliber.

"Gonna shoot or offer me some coffee?" I asked, shaking the water off my hat.

"Have to consider it a moment," he answered with a chuckle. The sheriff eventually opened a desk drawer and put the pistol away. "Oh, go ahead and pour yourself a cup," he added, shrugging. "And stop shaking water all over the place."

"Don't want me to ruin such fine furniture?" I quipped.

"So," the sheriff asked, ignoring my remark, "did you find him?"

I took a long sip of the coffee and nodded. "He's outside."

"Do I have to hurry?" Finley asked. I suspected he already knew the answer.

I shook my head slowly. "Not on his account, you don't."

Jake Finley and I had known each other for a few years. Back in 1860 he and I had worked together on the Bar-Double-D spread, pushing cattle and wrangling horses. Jake was close to my age, or maybe even a year or two older. I never really asked him. At the time we worked together, we were still teenagers so a lot of the older hands used to kid us. Because there is safety in numbers we sort of hung together.

Back then Jake was sparking a pretty little thing named Marie Alcott. I remember her name even today because her father ran the local gun shop and I was always hanging around, trying to learn as much as I could about firearms. The fact that she was blonde and blue-eyed didn't hurt any, either, but Jake was sweet on her and I didn't believe in cutting in on a friend's territory. At least that's how I remember it.

The Bar-Double-D was run by the O'Connell family and was a fairly large ranch. It was so big, in fact, that it had several cabins built at the various extremes of its range so cowhands could stay overnight rather than have to ride back late at night or camp out in the rain. Sometimes we had long, hard chores assigned to us such as mending fences or branding cattle that could take several days, so those line cabins came in right handy.

One time Jake and I were over on the north forty when we found a steer that had been brought down by a puma. While losing stock to wildlife isn't all that unusual, what with all the wolves, bears, and such, this time it made us sit up and take notice. The tracks of this particular cat were special as there was an extra toe on both of the two rear paws.

Jake and I had both heard the stories around the bunkhouse and in town of an immensely large cougar with extra toes that had hunted this range for years. He had evaded all attempts to trap or shoot him. The locals called him Old Shredder because the carcasses of his prey had all been shredded to pieces.

"I'd sure like to get that cat in my sights," Jake had said that evening back in the cabin.

"Wow. That's the first time I heard you talk about anything other than Marie," I had joked.

"Think about it, Badger," Jake had said, ignoring my comment. "They've been hunting that cat for years and they've all come up empty-handed. Every single time."

"So?"

"Well, I don't know about you, but I'm getting downright tired of all those bunkhouse jokes."

I had shrugged my shoulders. "I try to ignore them. They're harmless enough."

"I don't care. I don't like 'em," Jake had replied. "But just think about it. If we get that cat, the other men will have to look at us differently. They'll end up saying . . . look, there go the two men who got Old Shredder!"

I had smiled at him. "Yeah, I'll have to admit that would be nice, wouldn't it?"

Oh, the innocence of youth.

For the rest of the night Jake and I had planned our hunt. We had decided to leave at dawn and to ride the high ground. The idea was to split up. One of us would climb as high as he could and work his way down while the other would work his way up. That way we would trap the cat between us.

Admittedly there was some risk in the plan besides the obvious one presented by the big cat. For one thing, with one man above and one below we might end up shooting in each other's direction. Both of us realized that and decided it was still worth the risk. We also agreed that if we got Old Shredder, we would share the credit, regardless of who made the kill shot.

We drew straws and I got the short one, so Jake got to choose, deciding he'd go high and work down. Come morning, I'd be working my way uphill.

As planned we started climbing early. Actually I was doing all the climbing and as far as I was concerned it seemed to be all straight up. Jake on the other hand was riding his buckskin behind the hills where trails lead up and around. The plan was for him to tie his horse up as high in the hills as possible and then work his way down.

On this side of the Bar-Double-D the hills had a lot of caves, and, as I was climbing, it occurred to me that the cat could be hiding in any one of them. All it would take would be a swipe from one of his paws to send me flying down that cliff. I had my rifle slung over my shoulder. The idea was to reach a certain rock shelf about halfway up the hill. If the cat didn't show by then, I'd start making noise and try to drive it upward into Jake's sights.

It never occurred to us that instead of retreating back up the hill that cat might actually attack downward. That stupid little miscalculation almost cost me my life.

I reached the shelf without incident and waited. I didn't carry a watch so I can only estimate the amount time I sat watching the pockmarked hillside for signs of movement. It must have been about three hours before I finally spotted Jake, standing up at the crest of the hill.

I got ready to shoot and then started screaming. I fired my rifle in the air. All that ruckus was intended to spook the cat, but instead of charging up the hill right into Jake's sights as we'd planned, Old Shredder bolted out of the crevice he'd been hiding in and came downhill, jumping from rock to rock, so that Jake never had a chance to get a bead on him.

Back then, my rifle was a single-shot, not a repeater, and I was still in the process of reloading when the cougar leaped right for me. Trust me, there is nothing as terrifying as the thought of being eaten. Well, that's not precisely true. The one thing that is more terrifying is actually being eaten.

Old Shredder was huge and more than lived up to his reputation. That cat landed right on top of me, knocking me backward. He slashed my right shoulder, and, as I raised my forearm to protect myself, he bit down hard on it. Jake fired but the shot missed. In hindsight that shot was, to say the least, pretty stupid since I was positioned right under the cat. I don't really remember what happened next because I had already passed out.

According to what Jake later told me—and I now take anything he says with a grain of salt— his shot, even though it missed, chipped a nearby rock. Supposedly the rock chips ricocheted and scared the cat. Personally I don't think anything could scare that cat. Then, as Jake tells it, Old Shredder let out a growl and bounded away downhill against a hail of gunfire from Jake. How the hell he produced a hail of gunfire is beyond me since he carried a single-shot rifle like I did.

Regardless of what Jake's shot really did or why Old Shredder decided to run instead of chew me to pieces, when I woke up, I found myself spread-eagled over my horse. Jake had managed to secure a rope and then lower me down off that rock shelf. Eventually he got me over to my horse, and then led me back to the cabin. He tended to my wound and poured some "Who Hit Joe" down me. He stayed with me for three full days until I was well enough to sit a saddle. Now that I think about it, I realize that Jake may have been so considerate because he felt guilty about how everything had turned out. Regardless of his reasons I was still grateful to him.

When we made it back to the ranch, we related exactly what had happened to the other cowhands. As they heard the story, I was walking from the cabin over to the brook to fill my canteen when the cat pounced on me from out of nowhere. I fought him tooth and claw but Old Shredder was enormous. Had it not been for Jake hearing my cries and heroically shooting on the run and scaring him away, I'd have been a goner for sure. Leastwise that's how we told it.

Chapter Six

The lawman got up from his desk and walked to the window. Looking out, he saw the chestnut mare with a long burlap-wrapped body draped over its back.

"You ever bring one back alive, Badger?" Jake asked.

"Never been up to me," I responded angrily. "Anyone that wants to give up peaceably gets treated fairly. Problem is, the sort I get sent after don't seem to act . . . what ya might call . . . reasonably."

"Seems like there might be at least one or two that would," the sheriff remarked sarcastically.

"Let me put it this way," I replied. "Any of the men on those Wanted posters of yours currently sleeping in the town's hotel?"

Jake Finley went over to the stove and poured himself a cup of coffee. After taking a sip, he shook his head and answered: "Not a chance. And if they were, it would be a very short nap before they suddenly found themselves back here in a locked cell." He nodded toward the rear of his jail.

"I don't doubt it for a moment," I said honestly. "But what if they don't want to come along peacefully? What if they put up a fight? What then?"

The lawman answered proudly. "Then they'd have to answer to me and . . ." He paused.

"Your firearms?" I asked.

Perturbed, Sheriff Finley frowned at me. "But every one?"

"Coincidence. Them's only the ones you've seen. You're not the only lawman in the West that I deal with, ya know."

"I hope not," he replied.

"Now, about the reward money," I said, handing him a Wanted poster I had pulled out of my coat pocket. "Oh, and let's not forget the body. That mare's getting a mite tired after lugging it all this way."

Finley walked back to his desk, opened a drawer, and removed a notepad. He picked up a pencil, wet it with his tongue, and wrote some-thing down. "Take this chit to the bank and they'll pay you off," he explained.

I took the note and smiled. "Don't you want to examine the deceased for identification pur-poses?" I asked.

Sheriff Finley smiled. "I'll get to it later, but, in spite of your less than desirable line of work, I've never known you to make a mistake yet. Especially if there was a buck in it."

"Especially if," I agreed.

I walked over to the weapons rack and removed my holster.

As I was buckling it on, the sheriff opened his desk drawer and removed his Colt. "Let me ask you this, Badger. Why the hell don't you get yourself a real sidearm?" He twirled the pistol. "Faster on the draw than that sawed-off and carries six rounds in a pinch instead of just the two."

I removed my hat and rubbed my head before replacing it.

"All these years and I never told you before?" I asked.

Jake shook his head. "Nope. Never brought it up."

I thought out my reply. "Since I was a kid, I've always had a problem seeing far and to make matters worse during the war I took a Minié ball to the head. Ever since then I've had some eye-hand co-ordination problems on the right side. I'd fumble if I had to get cute with a small pistol." I patted the shotgun. "Hard to miss up close with this."

The lawman nodded. "All right, I'll buy that, but if, as you say, you don't see well up close, what about at a distance? Shotgun ain't much use unless you're close."

I picked up the Springfield from the corner and reached into the inside lining of my coat. I pulled out a small telescopic sniper's sight. With a snap and twist it locked into place on top of the rifle.

"Even with plain iron sights, this Springfield will hit well out to a thousand yards, and with a telescopic sight I have a fighting chance to see what I'm aiming at," I explained. "I can practically read the fine print on a Bible at seven hundred and fifty yards."

"I doubt you'd even recognize the Good Book if you saw one." Finley replied. "But at least try one of the newer repeaters. They hold more firepower than that single-shot breech-loader."

"Yep, they do. But they are harder for me to load and working the lever in a hurry is more of a chore for me," I answered. "Also the Forty-Five-Seventy cartridge packs more of a wallop than the Thirty-Thirty most of the repeaters use. This puts them down and keeps them down. So far this combination has kept me alive and I see no reason to change now."

The lawman just shrugged. "Just trying to help. It's your funeral."

"Not yet it ain't," I replied. "Take it slow, Jake. I'd appreciate it if you'd have my mule put in the livery stable next to my Appaloosa after you're done with the body."

"Will do," he said.

"Oh, and any reason you know of why I can't

keep that mare of his?" I asked. "Got a mite attached to her on the trip."

Jake shook his head. "None I can think of. He don't have any next of kin that I know about and I guess you earned it. By the way, where you headed?"

I rubbed my hand over my mouth. "Well, for now, I'll probably just head over to the saloon and have a beer. Then I plan to hit the hotel, clean up a mite, and have dinner."

"A shave wouldn't hurt none, either," he observed. "You gonna stay in town long?" he asked.

I laughed. "Don't worry, Mister Sheriff, sir. I'm planning to leave in the morning. Heading back to my ranch. I'm gonna relax for a while and that's a promise," I said sarcastically.

Jake Finley looked relieved. Maybe a little too relieved, I thought sadly, especially considering it came from someone I generally held out to be a friend.

"Watch your back, ol' son," he offered kindly.

"Always do," I said, tipping my hat brim. " 'Bye, Jake."

I removed the brass telescopic sight from the rifle and slid it into an inside pocket. When I walked outside, I immediately noticed the rain had subsided. Even though I wasn't a big fan of town living, it seemed to me that it might turn out to be a pleasant evening, after all.

Chapter Seven

I had just finished a long and arduous trek, trailing after a miserable low-life bank robber who had shot a Wells, Fargo agent for no apparent reason, even after he had already been given the money. He was a coward and a thief, but I had to hand it to him, when it came to the Owl Hoot Trail he was no fool and proved skittish enough to make things difficult.

It took me almost two months to find his track and to work my way around in front of him before the man finally rode into my sights. I wasn't lying to Sheriff Finley, either. I gave the outlaw a fair chance to surrender, but he threw a shot at me that almost hit my horse, and then took off at a gallop. Fortunately a .45-70 rifle shell does a pretty fair job of stopping someone from doing whatever it is they're doing at the time.

With the $750 reward promised from the WANTED ALIVE OR DEAD poster, I knew I'd be able to make quite a few improvements on my ranch back in the foothills of the Medicine Bow Mountains and maybe even add some new livestock. By all rights things in general should have been looking up for a good long while.

Funny thing is, I'd noticed that whenever you come into good weather there always seems to be a thunderstorm just over the horizon. Seems to me every pat on the back I ever got was followed almost immediately by a kick in the pants.

I took a deep breath, coughed a little to clear my throat, and then turned away from the jail and headed toward the saloon. I couldn't have gone more than a half a dozen steps when I heard a loud, angry voice behind me.

"Hey you, stranger!" the voice called.

I turned slowly, carefully cocking the hammer back on the Springfield rifle.

"This mangy mutt belong to you?" he asked.

In my line of work it pays to notice as much as you can about people. I judged the man who was facing me to be in his late twenties. He was clean-shaven, had long brown hair, was somewhat short of stature but stocky. He was bent over slightly and holding his left leg down near the shin as if in pain. I noticed he carried a skinning knife in a sheath on his right hip and a Richards-Mason Model 1850 Army Colt .44 pistol stuck through his belt on the left side with the butt end facing to the right, cross-draw style.

I'd seen a lot of pistols like that in the last few years. Apparently this Richards fellow along with a man named William Mason had worked out a way of taking old black powder percussion cap Army and Navy pistols and reworking them to accept rear-loading metallic cartridges. These pistols were easy to recognize because the loading lever was replaced by an ejector rod. Richards and Mason added a breech plate with a firing pin and a rear sight mounted on it. The word was that these same two men were the gents responsible for the design of the new Colt six-shot pistol everyone had taken to calling a Peacemaker. Whoever they were, my hat was off to them for their gun savvy.

"I asked you if this filthy beast belongs to you?" the man repeated rudely.

I looked down at Lobo, who was still lying at the rail next to my horse, and shrugged.

"Don't know as how he belongs to me," I replied, "but he does like to follow me around wherever I go. Still, all and all he tends to be a fairly independent sort. That answer your question?"

The man rubbed his left leg and then straightened up. He walked up to me and started pointing his finger at me. "That stupid mutt just bit me," he stated angrily.

"Down there on your leg?" I asked.

"Yeah, and what are you gonna do about it?"

"Usually there are two ways people get bit," I said. "One is on the hand or arm when they reach down to pet or grab a dog. Second is on the leg and that mostly happens when you try to kick 'em. That what happened, mister?"

He paused a moment as if sizing me up. "What if it was? He was blocking my way."

I looked around him and back at Lobo who was still lying there at the edge of the sidewalk. As I could have predicted, he never for a moment took his eyes off the stranger.

"Oh, I highly doubt that. Seems like there's plenty of room," I answered. "You got a name?"

"Wilkins," he replied angrily.

"Well, Mister Wilkins," I continued, "next time I suggest you walk around him."

"The hell I will!" he exclaimed angrily. He was still shaking his finger in my face. "You're gonna pay for this."

Before this conversation got any more aggravating, I grabbed his right index finger with my left hand, pushed it backward, and bent it almost in half down toward his body. The response was about as I'd expected. He screamed and bent forward just as the butt of my rifle stock was traveling upward from my right. He went down like he was pole-axed.

I looked down at him to make sure he wasn't dead, and then over at Lobo and yelled out: "Two seconds! We're in town two seconds and already you're making trouble." Lobo just looked up with that half smile of his and barked once. His tail never stopped wagging the whole time.

"Better come with me so he don't shoot you when he wakes up." I carefully lowered the hammer on my rifle, and then waved my hand to him. "Here, boy."

The massive dog jumped up as if I were a rabbit and followed me down the street to the nearest saloon. I looked back to make sure he didn't mark his territory on the man's body. I don't know where he picked up that little trick but I figured that at least for now enough was enough.

Chapter Eight

The Tomahawk Saloon was hardly what you would call elegant but it certainly was busy. It was conveniently located halfway down the main street of town, and while that location definitely helped with business, the main draw was the fact that the place had a stage in the middle of it with a three-piece band and a chorus of five women who all sang. If you could call their caterwauling singing, that is. They also danced some without falling over much. The patrons really seemed to enjoy the show, but then again most of them were usually drunk. Truthfully, if you were sober, the sight of that chorus line would probably make you shudder.

Oh, sure, I'll freely admit I'm no great shakes to look at, but the faces on these lovely ladies would not only stop a clock, they'd make the hands go backward.

Disregarding the possible consequences I pushed myself through the bat-wing doors and held them open to allow Lobo to follow me in. I found a corner near the front door that was unoccupied and motioned for him to hunker down there. "Down and stay," were the only commands I needed. I can assure you, we had been through this routine many times before.

Someone watched us enter and addressed me in a rather gruff tone. "I don't think they allow dogs in here," he remarked.

I looked him over quickly and then just stared him in the eyes without saying a word. He tried to hold my gaze for a moment, and then dropped his eyes. That's when I knew there would be no more problems on his account.

"But I guess they'd make an exception for your dog," he said somewhat timidly. I just nodded back at him. "Besides," he added, "it ain't no skin offen my nose. I ain't the owner here."

"No, you're not," I agreed. I walked right past him and over to the bar and never glanced back. It's not that I took anything for granted, but sometimes it's best not to let them see you sweat, as they say. Besides, the crowd's reaction to anything out of the ordinary and the large mirror in front of me would have tipped me of any potential problem.

"What'll ya have, mister?" the bartender asked.

"Something to calm both the thirst and the spirit," I replied, leaning the Springfield upright next to my leg at the bar.

"Beer it is, then." He smiled. "Just tapped a fresh keg."

"Sure you did." I laughed.

The barkeep seemed to be in his fifties and wore one of those long, waxed handlebar mustaches. What little hair he had on his head was combed straight back and held in place with hair slick. He had a big belly that wasn't totally hidden by the greasy apron he wore. In general, though, he seemed a pleasant enough fellow. He grabbed a glass mug off a pile of them and walked over to the tap. After wiping the glass with his apron, he filled the mug to the top with just the right amount of suds and slid the glass down the bar.

"Catch," he said. "Show's about to start in a moment."

I nodded my head. "Sure wouldn't want to miss that now, would I?" I replied.

"You been here before, I'd guess," he remarked, chuckling.

"On occasion." I nodded again with a smile.

"Well, they may not be much to look at, but they is pure female."

"Pure?" I asked.

"Well, female at any rate," he said, grinning. "Name's George, if ya need anything else." He turned to help another customer, and I turned the other way, facing toward the stage.

The musicians were already in place and had begun playing what I believe was an old Irish tune called "The Minstrel Boy." People in the saloon were moving around in order to get a better view of the show and waiters were carrying trays over their heads loaded with mugs of beer, whiskey glasses, and the occasional plate of sliced jerky.

I settled back and began to relax. The atmosphere in the Tomahawk was always lively and not too rowdy for my taste. I took a long swallow of beer and had to admit that George may have been telling the truth about it being a fresh keg. Or maybe I was just thirsty. Either way, it was just fine.

I had just set the glass down on the bar and was turning to order another when there was a shout and the saloon doors burst open.

"Where is he? Where is that low life son-of-a-bitch?" someone yelled.

I turned quickly to see that man who called himself Wilkins barge through the door. Our eyes locked and he went for the pistol in his belt. One of the women in the room screamed and I knew my rifle would be of little use. It was too hard to get to and I simply didn't have enough time. I would have gone for my scatter-gun but he drew that hogleg of his with incredible speed. There was no way with my limitations I could match his draw.

"Lobo! Gun!" I yelled.

The big dog, that had been resting right next to

those doors, sprang up at the man and sank his teeth into his forearm just behind the pistol. A single shot rang out, but fortunately Lobo's attack had deflected Wilkins's aim up and over to the left. The bullet just shattered a lamp hanging on the wall without hitting anyone in the crowd.

I don't rightly know how a wolf bite compares to a dog's bite but in this case I suspect the man got the worst of both worlds. Hell, I wouldn't be surprised if the bone didn't snap. At any rate he dropped the revolver quicker than a hot potato. The pain was so great the scream stuck in his throat.

"Lobo! Leave!" I commanded. Had I not given the command he would have ripped the man's arm off and then proceeded to do the same with the rest of his worthless body. "Leave" was his off command. I'd figured out over the years that when someone is bitten, they'll usually yell something like "Stop it!" or "Get off!" By using the word "Leave" instead as a command, I could almost guarantee that I would be the only one controlling that big wolf hybrid.

As I expected, Lobo let go and came to my side. Wilkins was stooped over and holding his bloody arm. The pain on his face told me I had no need for my gun. I just walked over and booted him through the door and into the street. I turned back to the bar and retrieved the rifle. Motioning to George the barman I tossed some coins on the bar. "That should cover the drinks and the lamp. Sorry about all the fuss."

"No problem," George responded. "It was obvious he drew first. By the way, that's some dog you have there. Never saw one quite that big."

"He's half wolf," I explained.

"Handy to have around," he said admiringly.

"Oh, you have no idea." I turned, and before walking out the door I stopped to pick up the six-shooter Wilkins had dropped. Once out in the street I walked right into Sheriff Finley who was helping Wilkins to his feet.

"I heard a shot. What in the Sam Hill is going on here?" Jake asked angrily.

Before I could reply Wilkins whimpered out. "He started it. First his dog bit me right outside your office, and then he butted me with that damn' rifle o' his. I was just trying to get even."

"That true, Badger?" the lawman asked.

"Not exactly. He drew a finger on me first," I explained, handing the pistol over to the sheriff.

"Well, if that's the case . . . wait . . . he drew a what?"

"A finger," I reiterated calmly. "Stuck it right there in my face. I never liked that much. As for the bite, I expect Lobo was just protecting himself from being kicked by a bully."

Jake looked at me with squinted eyes and shook his head. "A finger. Well if that don't beat all. Look, Badger, you said you were planning on leaving in the morning. Make sure it happens. All right?"

I merely nodded in agreement.

"As for you," he said, turning to the injured man, "hand over that knife and then get yourself over to Doc Higgins. Have him fix you up, and then as soon as you can, and I mean right *pronto*, get on your horse and get out of town."

"What about my gun and knife?" Wilkins asked.

Jake looked at me and I just shrugged.

"Swing by my office on your way out of town. I'll escort you to the town limits, and then I'll give them back. But not before then. Understood?"

The man pulled his knife out slowly and passed it over to the sheriff, handle first. Last I saw of him he was holding his arm and trailing drops of blood down the street.

"Not a half hour in town and already there's a problem," Jake commented wryly. "Now I got to go saddle my horse and escort this lowlife out of town. Gonna miss my afternoon nap."

I'd never seen Jake Finley take a nap in all the years I'd known him.

"Sorry," I replied. "But it's like I said, Jake, he pulled a finger on me."

The lawman shook his head. As he walked away, I pondered the conversation we'd had back in his office. Ever since I was a kid my right side seemed numb from the shoulder down. My

fingers tingled from time to time and I had a
weak grip. My eyesight wasn't what it should be
when compared to others my age, either. Things
were a little fuzzy at far distances, and worse
so since I took that Minié ball to the head in
1864. Over the years the sawed-off had always
provided a solution to those issues. After all, it's
hard to miss with a scatter-gun.

Chapter Nine

Things had been changing quickly in the last few
years. Back when everyone was using percussion caps and single-shot pistols, the weapons I
carried always proved good enough for my
personal needs. Lately, however, there seemed
to be a repeater on everyone's hip. And it wasn't
just the firearms that were changing.

A good many men were sporting those new
holster designs with the belt riding lower for a
faster draw. Some had cut-downs on the holster's
front side to speed things up when pulling the
pistol out. Hell, with a slight hammer and trigger
modification a gunslick could empty all six
shots from a Colt Single-Action Army practically
before you heard the first one go off.

Jake wasn't the only one who realized the
advantage of a fast repeater, but I hadn't figured
out a solution to the problem yet. I'd have to

ruminate some more on it. I headed over to the stable where the Appaloosa had been put up and retrieved my saddlebags and duffel. There I made arrangements to have the horses and the mule cared for the way I wanted and made sure Lobo would be put up for the night with something to eat.

Usually I just turned him loose to run off and hunt on his own, often for days at a time, but with all the trouble we'd gotten into I wanted him secured for the night. Once that was taken care of, I started reëvaluating the events of the day. As I walked toward the hotel, I continued to ponder the problem of how to hold on to my professional edge with the weapons of choice I carried.

That was when I passed by the general store, or the Shebang as it was called locally. I stepped in for a moment to buy a couple cigars and it was then that I noticed the clerk pouring some lemonade into a cup for one of the customers' kids. Apparently the store offered the lemonade drink as a free incentive in order to attract family business.

It wasn't the lemonade that attracted my attention, however. It was the pitcher that was being used. I had seen these types of set-ups before in fancy hotels but they were usually reserved for tea or coffee. In essence it was a curved frame with a swivel that held the pot. Rather than having to lift and carry the coffee by a hot handle every time, all a waiter had to do was put the cup under the spout and incline the pot. The pot would swivel down, pour out the coffee, and then would be returned to its original upright position. I thought it kind of clever that the store-keeper had rigged his lemonade pitcher with the same idea to save time and avoid messy spills. It also gave me a hell of an idea.

When I left the store, I looked around for a leather smith or saddle shop. Down the street at the very end of the first series of shops was a sign that indicated just what I needed. It simply read: SADDLE REPAIR. I adjusted the saddlebags on my shoulder and walked straight over there.

Just as I'd hoped, the owner, a gent named Murphy, indicated that he could fix just about anything that had rawhide or leather, be it cinch, saddle, belt, or bag. I set the duffel and the Springfield down against the wall next to the door and spent a few minutes explaining what I had in mind. Finally the man caught the drift of what I wanted.

"Leave me that belt and holster of yours and give me till morning. I think I can work it out for you by then, mate."

"Just as long as it's ready by morning," I replied, "and I'll be most grateful. You need the scattergun, too?" I asked. "I'd feel a little naked without it."

"Shouldn't think so," he answered, shaking his head. He took out a small receipt book and looked up. "What name should I put this under?"

"Jedidiah Kershaw. Most folks just call me Badger, though."

The leather smith looked a little puzzled. "Badger? That's a new one," he remarked. "How'd you get that handle, if you don't mind my asking?"

I shook my head and took no offense. I'd heard the question many times before. "Some say it's 'cause once I get hold of something, I don't let go. Others say it's 'cause I got a mean streak that comes out when I'm forced to back up." Mr. Murphy looked a mite uncomfortable, so I added: "I was tagged with it as a kid and I guess it just stuck. Easier than Jedidiah."

Mr. Murphy relaxed and smiled. "Very well . . . Mister Kershaw, this will be ready by . . . say nine a.m.?"

"Great. Any reason you need me, I'll be over at the hotel," I said. And after retrieving my rifle and duffel, that's where I headed next.

Chapter Ten

The Turnberry Hotel was one of three places to stay in the town of Cooper's Crossing, but it was the only one where I was fairly certain I wouldn't catch any bedbugs. I walked through the front door and was immediately surprised at all the changes the proprietor had made since I had last been there. In the center of the lobby was a large, round, red velvet-covered couch that was new, and I noticed that the place had been freshly wallpapered.

I walked up to the front desk, set my tack down, and rang the bell that was sitting on the counter. A young man who couldn't have been more than fifteen or so walked out from the back room and offered his help. He wore a white shirt with suspenders and had on a name badge that read PETE.

"A room for just one night," I stated. "Still serving dinner here?"

Pete nodded. "Best pot roast in town and tonight we have beef barley soup and apple pie for dessert. Fresh, too."

"I should hope so." As I replied, my stomach rumbled a bit. I looked down and rubbed my belly. "Sounds like just what the doctor ordered."

"Please sign here," he said, indicating a line in his registry.

"A sign-in book," I observed. "Getting real upscale, aren't we?"

Pete looked at me sheepishly. "Pa, I mean Mister Turnberry, says it helps the place run more efficiently. Keeps track of where folks are, getting the right room and such."

I chuckled. "Well, Pete, your pappy is probably right. Wouldn't want someone accidentally walking in on Mister and Missus Finnigan before they got to begin again, now, would we?" I joked.

The lad seemed a little perplexed. "Never mind," I added, shrugging. "Just point me to the room."

"Upstairs two flights. Third door on the right." Pete handed me a ring with two keys on it. "Bathroom is at the other end of the hall on the far left," he explained. "That's why there's a second key."

"A lock on the bathroom door, too," I said, surprised. "Now I know we've come up in the world." I threw the saddlebags back over my shoulder, once more picked up the duffel and rifle, and walked up the stairs.

After a long bath, a shave, and a change of not-so-clean clothes I headed down to the dining hall. The smell of food drew me like a Sonora steer to a watering hole. The crowded room indicated to me the food must still be as good as I remembered it to be.

I left the Springfield up in the hotel room but carried the sawed-off under the jacket that was draped over my arm. I hoped it would be less conspicuous that way. Almost everyone was armed in one way or another, from pocket Derringers to Winchesters, but I noticed that when pistols and other short-barreled firearms were carried out of their holsters, it tended to make folks uneasy. The last thing I wanted was to attract any more attention in Jake's town.

I found a table in the corner and placed the express gun across my lap and set a large napkin over it. A rather substantially built, blonde waitress came over and smiled. "Are you waiting for someone or shall I take your order now?" she asked politely.

I took off my hat and placed it on the seat next to me. "You on the menu?" I asked.

She giggled and punched me gently in the shoulder. "I'll take that to mean you're alone."

"You didn't answer my question," I replied, smiling.

"Not officially," she answered, looking me over. "But you never know. Might be as how things could change later." She winked.

"Gee, I sure hate to wait," I said honestly, "but for now I'll have the soup and pot roast. Word is they're serving apple pie for dessert."

"Best pie in four counties," she replied proudly, while tossing back her hair. Aside from being blonde, young, and well put together, as they say, I also noticed she had very pretty blue eyes. Then again, I'd been out on the trail alone for several months.

"Does it come with cheese on it?" I asked

"Well, you know what they say," she teased.

"What's that?" I asked, perplexed.

"Apple pie without cheese is like a hug without a squeeze." She laughed. By this point I was even more convinced that pie wouldn't be my only dessert.

"Right," I said. "And hot coffee with all that."

"Coming right up," she said, heading for the kitchen. I couldn't help noticing that her train had a noticeable wiggle in its caboose.

Dinner lived up to its expectations, and that included the apple pie with cheese.

"Here's your check, sir," she said, handing me the bill.

"Put it on my room tab," I said, taking the pencil gently from behind her ear. "I'm writing my room number right here in big letters so you can find it easy enough." I smiled as harmlessly as I could. Sort of like a mongoose smiling to a cobra. "And just call me Badger, most of my friends do."

She punched me in the shoulder again. "My, you are a devil, aren't ya?"

"And a very hopeful one to boot," I added with a chuckle.

"Keep the faith, Badger. One never knows what fortune the future may bring," she replied, smiling.

"Well, seeing as how I'm leaving in the morning, I can only hope the future don't take very long."

I waited until she had left the table before removing the napkin and getting up. I carried the scatter-gun concealed snugly against my leg as I headed back to my room. On my way up the stairs I began to wonder whether I truly wanted that special knock on the door, or if deep down I would really prefer a chance to get a good night's sleep in a comfortable indoor bed.

Chapter Eleven

Once I was back in my hotel room, I placed the sawed-off under the bed and took a look around. It didn't need any sprucing up. The staff of the Turnberry seemed to have done a competent job. They had even folded the little towels next to the wash pot so they had triangular points on the end.

A bounty man doesn't often spend much time in highfaluting establishments, but that doesn't mean he doesn't appreciate high toning it when he gets the chance. The room was decorated with a high-backed cane-bottom chair and a small writing desk next to it. There was the wash basin with the little towels and a bed with a small brass headboard. It had a fairly thick mattress on it, too, a far cry from the cots the Army used to supply us with. There were two lamps hung on the walls and a large painting of what I assumed was an Eastern farmhouse. Western ranches seldom have fringed surreys out front and lanes edged with roses and posies.

I laughed out loud when I remembered that the last hotel room I was in had a tobacco poster nailed to the wall that was riddled with bullet holes.

I plopped down on the bed and pulled off my boots. I favored the high black cavalry officers' model boots although I never did rise above corporal during all my years of service. After unbuttoning my shirt, I leaned back. I was almost about to fall asleep when there was a soft knocking at the door. I noticed that the small pendulum clock on the wall indicated 9:00 p.m. I got up, admittedly somewhat reluctantly, and walked to the door. I repositioned the Springfield Trapdoor behind the door and asked who it was.

"It's Betty," she replied. "Come on, sweets, open the door afore I catch a draft."

I opened it slightly. In my line of work it pays to be careful and I had only just met this girl. Happily she was alone and carrying a bottle of wine to boot.

I smiled widely and opened the door. "Well, come in and be my guest, said the spider to the fly."

"Oh, you are terrible, aren't you." She giggled.

A gentleman never kisses and tells but I've never been accused of being excessively gentlemanly. Needless to say we had a few drinks and then settled down to getting to know each other. It must have been about a half hour later when we heard a loud commotion coming from out back of the hotel, apparently right under my window.

I sat up and began to get out of bed to see what was afoot.

"Oh, must you?" Betty whined. "Things was just getting interesting."

The noise got louder. It sounded like barrels being knocked over and men yelling at one another. I rose and went over to look out the window. Or more precisely let's just say I looked around the window sill. I didn't lean out or anything like that. This child wasn't raised that dumb. When I did peer out that window a couple of shots rang out.

I noticed a group of three obviously drunken men staggering down the street, and raising the roof. One of them chucked a small barrel through one of the storefront windows and the other two were firing their pistols in the air. Off to my left I saw Sheriff Finley walking toward them. He had a Winchester '73 cradled in his arms.

I went over to the chair where I had draped my jacket and retrieved the telescopic sight from its pocket. I quickly returned to the window and looked more closely through the glass.

"What's happening, sweetie?" Betty asked, adjusting her hair.

"Oh, it looks like the sheriff's got his hands full with some local ruffians," I answered.

"Jake can take care of himself," she observed. "That man's a handful all by his lonesome, I'd say."

I looked over at her and winked. "Kinda like me?"

She merely giggled. "Ya jealous, sweetie?"

I went back to watching the street and heard

the sheriff shout. "Not in my town, boys! That'll be enough for tonight."

Apparently they weren't having any of it because they began to spread apart, and then squared off in front of him.

"Yeah? Who says?" one of them asked.

"The law, and that's all you need to know. Just go somewhere and sober up. Not much harm done yet."

"And iffen we don't want to go?" another asked.

At this point I motioned to Betty. "Hand me that rifle, would you?"

"Rifle?" she cried. "Hey, what ya gonna do?" She was obviously beginning to worry, but she brought me the Springfield anyway.

"I hope nothing," I responded. "But it pays to be prepared."

"Prepared? For what? Hey, what exactly's going on out there?" she asked nervously.

"Just stay back away from the window," I replied sternly.

I squatted down and brought the rifle to rest on the window sill and moved it slowly to and fro watching the scene on the street below.

Suddenly a man emerged from an alley farther off to the right with a long shotgun in his arms. I put my finger on the trigger and took a closer look through the scope. It was then I noticed the badge on the man's chest. I breathed a sigh of relief.

"Friends, let me introduce you to my new

deputy. His name's Jessie. Been with me just a short time now, but, trust me, he's been using that shotgun of his for a long, long time," Jake explained, just loud enough for me to overhear. "He's real good with it."

"So Jake's gone and got religion," I mused out loud.

"How's that?" Betty asked.

"It's about time he got some help," I said to myself as much as to Betty. "This town's grown too big for just one lawman and Jake takes too many chances as far as I'm concerned."

I adjusted the rifle. Even with the appearance of the deputy I couldn't help feeling that something was wrong. Call it a sort of sixth sense. By now those men, even drunk as they were, should have changed their attitude. Facing a Winchester in front and a shotgun to the side would make any man a believer. I knew something was up. There was no back-up at all showing in those men.

"You go to hell!" one of the group yelled. "And that goes for your play pal, too."

Once again I swept the area with the scope that was now mounted on my rifle. It was then that I noticed a sixth man crouched in the shadows back behind the deputy.

"How about it, boys? Shall we show these citified town-building peckerwoods how it's done back home?"

Everything seemed to happen at once. The man

in the shadows stood up and I held my sights right over his chest as I pulled the trigger. A .45-70 bullet can take down a buffalo at that range, and what it did to that man was more than sufficient to send him straight to Hades with a non-stop train ticket.

Betty screamed in my ear and about the same time down on the street the men facing the lawmen all drew their weapons. Since they were caught between a Winchester rifle and the shotgun there wasn't much point wondering if any of them had survived the encounter.

"What the hell?" Sheriff Finley shouted, spinning around.

I waved at him from the window.

"Well, I'll be damned," he said, looking up.

"Probably!" I shouted down.

"Jessie and I sure owe you one, Badger," he yelled, nudging the bodies one by one with the barrel of his rifle.

"You sure do!" I hollered down. "You interrupted a right pleasant evening." Remembering my roommate, I set the rifle down and turned to her. "Now, where were we?" I smiled.

She looked at me aghast. "You just shot him down without a warning!" she cried. "You murdered him from hiding without giving him a chance!"

"Just like he was going to do to the deputy," I observed. "What would you have me do? Mail him an invitation or wait till he blew away the law?" I asked, shaking my head in disgust.

She picked up what remained of the wine bottle and headed quickly to the door.

"Well," I said to her just before she stormed out. "I expect shootings do tend to put a damper on romance." She slammed the door on her way out.

I took the sniper sight off the rifle and put it away. Then I took a cleaning kit from a small compartment hidden in the back of the rifle stock and cleaned the rifle's bore. After that, I washed my face in the basin and went to bed. I guess that particular night sleeping won out over other activities, after all.

Chapter Twelve

The next morning I rose early and had a quick breakfast of ham and eggs with some extra hot black coffee. Betty was nowhere to be found, but given the prior night's events it wasn't surprising and that was all right with me. After settling my hotel bill, I headed over to the bank and cashed out the chit for my reward money. At about 9:00 I went over to Murphy's Saddle Repair.

"Good morning, Mister Kershaw," he said pleasantly. "I have just what you ordered all ready." Murphy walked over to his workbench and retrieved my belt and holster. He handed them to me, explaining: "It turned out to be a rather simple job, but I have to admit it is a clever idea."

I immediately noticed that he had embellished slightly over my original idea. The belt was no longer straight but rather over the area of the right hip he had sewn a thick U-shaped extra flap of leather onto the belt in order to allow the holster to ride a little lower. The buscadero-style boot-top holster that normally had a leather fold through which the cartridge belt passed had been replaced with a brass stud and bracket attachment that bolted the holster right into the now widened belt.

I turned the rig over in my hands. The side of the holster that made contact with the belt had an oversize brad, or brass button, pushed through the leather. There was also a small patch of leather sewed on in such a way as to cover the inside of the holster to prevent the metal brad from rubbing, catching, or scratching the scatter-gun. The actual belt had an indented brass bracket sewn into the flap into which the stud articulated while holding the holster in place. The whole affair was double-stitched and reinforced with a criss-cross pattern like you saw on the better grade of saddlery. I couldn't help but feel that it gave a little class to the whole affair.

"You polished it up, too," I noticed.

"No extra charge. I won't let leather go out of my

establishment without cleaning it," he commented.

"Charge or not, it is a very nice touch." My praise was genuine.

Mr. Murphy broke into a wide grin. "Actually it is a nice grade of leather you have there. Whoever made this originally knew what he was doing. Very well made and tanned appropriately. Not urine-tanned like they do down south." Murphy coughed uncomfortably and added: "Both the holster and belt, however, were rather dirty." He clearly was admonishing me.

I must have looked a little sheepish. "I do know better, but I get a mite lazy about saddle-soaping my tack."

"Lasts longer iffen you do," he explained. "Go ahead, put it on. I'd like to check the fit."

As expected the belt and holster, now a one-piece outfit, fit like a glove. If anything, it was more comfortable and rode a little lower on my right hip. "I'm more than pleased with the job," I said.

"Some of the stitches were coming apart so I redid them and I reinforced the lining," Murphy explained. "I replaced the tie-down lace, too. It was pretty worn."

"I saw that. Very nicely done, too, if I might add. Just what I'd ordered. You must have stayed up all night to finish this on time."

The leather smith shrugged his shoulders. "It took a little longer than usual but I liked your idea. Wanted to see if I could get done just what you wanted."

"Well, Mister Murphy, you outdid yourself, I'll say that," I replied sincerely. After paying the man, I went outside and headed for the stable. It was time to leave.

When I finally rode out of town, I paused a moment to look back. Sheriff Finley was standing in the middle of the street with his hand up as a gesture of farewell. I waved a good bye and turned back toward the road home. Trailing behind me was the jack mule, that chestnut mare I had recovered, and, of course, Lobo.

Once we cleared the town, I raised a hand and motioned. "Go hunt." Lobo looked up at me and then raced off. When he wanted to, he could outrun a horse. Ever since he was pup that dog-wolf mix had a solitary streak in him, and as soon as he was old enough, he took to disappearing for days on end. At first there were times when I worried he might not ever return, but he always did. Somehow or another he always managed to pick up my scent. Sometimes he'd arrive covered in cockleburs or sand spurs, and other times he'd be dripping wet.

Occasionally he'd show up with a bloody rabbit in his mouth and drop it on my bedroll like he was bringing home a trophy for me. Always he seemed happy to be back and I couldn't help but enjoy his company, especially during long and lonely evening hours. I had a currycomb in my pack, and after dark I'd spend an hour or two brushing him down. He seemed to enjoy it and it brought me a mindless distraction that helped pass the time.

Once in a while Lobo would hear some wolf howl and perk up his ears, but, unless I gave him the nod to—"Go hunt."—he'd stick around the camp. Funny thing is, even though he was half wolf, the Appaloosa and the mule seemed to get along fine with him. Occasionally I noticed they seemed actually to play with Lobo, with him nipping at their heels and the horses jumping sideways. They never stomped or kicked him, though. Not once. Even when it might look to others that Lobo was rough housing a little too much in earnest, they all got along. They had grown up together and after all these years together we'd all learned to live with each other's bothersome tendencies.

The ride back home took three weeks through some rather hard and rocky territory, but finally we were in sight of my ranch. I sat on the Appaloosa, looking down into a small valley nestled in the prettiest foothills you've ever seen. I had found the place before the war and had staked it out. It was my refuge, my retreat if you will, a place where I could forget about enemies, danger, or worldly woe.

Originally I had been riding north in response

to a job opportunity I'd heard of. Not many were willing to hire someone so young for anything that entailed any sort of responsibility or willing to offer good pay for that matter. John Eldridge, however, had been different. He'd started West as a young man with Coulter and had eventually gone his own way. He lived as a mountain man for a while, lived with the Indians for a few years, and eventually took up mining.

One morning during a thunderstorm he awoke with a start after lightning struck right next to his tent. When he peered out the tent flap, he saw it had hit a small but wide tree a few feet away. The tree had been split right up the middle and had toppled over. Curious, Eldridge went over to the stump and came across what prospectors call a Glory Hole. There were gold nuggets the size of peach pits all over the stump and in the hole.

Eldridge, who was never very fond of digging holes anyway, took the money and reinvested it in a horse-breeding operation in Colorado. He had spread the word that anyone who was a wrangler or a peeler was welcome regardless of age. By then I could sit anything with four legs, and since Eldridge had a reputation for paying well and on time, I was riding to join his spread.

One day along the way I noticed a rather large-size elk and rode off in search of some fresh meat. That elk led me uphill and down until I was so turned around I couldn't tell where we were, where we were going, or how we got there. Then as I crested this hill, I saw the small valley below. It was a secluded sea of grass, and everywhere you looked there was color, whether from primrose plants, or shooting stars, or purple thistles.

I liked the fact that it was so secluded and that the land had a lot of possibilities. Cattle or horses could be ranched here, and there was plenty of fertile ground for planting. I eventually was able to stake a claim on it, although it would be several years before I could actually get around to start working there.

As I sat astride the Appaloosa, I knew it was just a stretch of land but as far as I was concerned it was also a small patch of pure paradise. "We're home, boy," I said, nudging the horse on.

Three hours later, in late afternoon, I rode up to the front gate. It felt good to be home where I could finally relax for a spell. At least that's what I fully intended on doing.

Chapter Thirteen

"Yo, the house!" I yelled. I leaned over and opened the gate. Lobo bounded into the front yard and barked excitedly. I rode over to the small log-and-branch corral I'd built off to the left of the house and dismounted. I unsaddled the horses and the mule, and turned them all loose in the corral. For the moment I threw the saddles and tack over the corral railing and turned back to the house.

"Yo, the house!" I yelled again. "Hey, Sarge, you around?"

The front door opened and an older man wearing a weather-worn Army campaign hat emerged.

"Shut yer yap," he said gruffly. "I heared ya. Knew ya was coming since you was up on the bluff," he insisted. That didn't surprise me much since nothing ever seemed to escape Sarge's watchful eye. Or maybe it was some extra sense the older ex-Army man had developed over the years.

Sergeant Richard Hackworth had served in the military in one capacity or another for over forty-some years. He had had a long and highly unusual career. During the 1850s he traveled to some place in the Far East called Bangkok as part of a small military protection detail for one of our ambassadors, a man named Townsend Harris. Apparently he later accompanied the ambassador over to Japan, where in his free time, he trained with some of the Emperor's personal bodyguards.

Sarge learned to speak the Japper's lingo and added that to his command of Spanish and three or four American Indian tongues. Apparently he had some sort of natural affinity to learn other languages. When he finally returned to America, he was transferred around to different outposts and eventually ended up as top soldier in our outfit and the brigade's hand-to-hand combat instructor.

In the meantime I had grown up migrating all over the West, doing one thing or another until ending up in the Midwest. Even as young as I was, I found jobs loading freight and driving wagons. I hammered railroad spikes for a while, and then rode express. I tried my hand at mining for a few months, but finally ended up working as an ordinary cowhand.

I had just finished escorting a small herd to Chicago when the war broke out. I wanted to enlist but the Army considered that at sixteen I was still too young. I hung around the town for another year supporting myself by doing such odd jobs as driving ice carts or coal wagons. Then in 1862 I lied about my age and joined the Army. I was assigned to the 6th Illinois Cavalry. It was as fine a unit as ever was mustered.

I still painfully remember the first time the Sarge and I met. Our squad was sent over to a practice session to learn about fighting hand-to-hand without weapons. We all sat around a circle while the sergeant stood in the middle, talking to us about fighting.

"Thought we was gonna ride and shoot in this here cavalry," one particularly big recruit offered, "not wrassle around." If I remember correctly his name was Miles. "Besides, I already know how to box," he boasted.

"Great," the Sarge said, pointing to him. "Then thanks for volunteering." The soldier smiled and, as he was standing up, whispered to me: "Watch this. I've never been beaten yet." Miles walked into the center of the circle, squared off, and put his dukes up.

"You know all that Marquis de Queensberry stuff?" the sergeant asked innocently.

"Sure do," the soldier replied proudly. Miles turned his head slightly and winked at me as if to share a confidence.

"Well, then, anytime you're ready," the Sarge said with a come-on gesture.

The young recruit started to advance and swung a big haymaker at the instructor's head. Sergeant Hackworth simply leaned to one side to avoid the punch and then kicked the man in the shin with the inside edge of his boot. It sounded like a hammer hitting a two-by-four. Private Miles went down in excruciating pain, face first. From the sound of the kick and the expression on the recruit's face I hoped the sergeant hadn't broken the man's leg.

"You kicked me," the soldier whimpered, looking up from the ground.

"Sorry, but I never learned all them fancy rules." Turning to the group, the sergeant continued: "We teach fighting here. We don't host no sporting events. We are going into battle where there ain't no rules. Remember, all's fair in love and war, and where you're going there sure as hell won't be any love."

Not one soldier laughed. Reflecting on my own weaknesses, I decided right there and then that I'd stick to this man like glue until I learned all his tricks.

With all my experience out West, growing up on the trail, I was soon transferred to the scouting section of the unit. My group was tasked with riding point and scouting around. We had to avoid leading the brigade into ambushes and were often ordered to find new routes to take the troop into or out of battle. Nobody ever found out about my age, and after a year and a half I was promoted to corporal.

It seemed to most of us that the North was having a hard time of things and eventually the Union Army got bogged down around Vicksburg, an armed fortress built on a two-hundred-foot cliff high above the Mississippi. It had huge cannons that would sink any Union vessel on the river, going up or down.

In February of 1863 General Grant came up with a new strategy to conquer the city. While Union gunboats sneaked past the Rebel gunners at night, General W.T. Sherman would plan a way to co-ordinate an attack from the south with his troops.

Up to this point in the war, however, Rebel cavalry with such leaders as J.E.B. Stuart and

Nathan Bedford Forrest had made fools of us. Confederate cavalrymen patrolled the riverbank area and would sound the alarm if they even smelled a Yankee. General Grant decided he needed a Union cavalry troop to draw the Rebels away from Vicksburg.

Grant wanted men willing to take risks, to ride hard and strike fast. That described the Illinois brigade to perfection. Colonel Benjamin Grierson was tasked with destroying the Vicksburg and Jackson Railroad at Newton Station, Mississippi. The mission that later became known as Grierson's Raid commenced on April 17th, 1863. The 6th and 7th Illinois rode out from La Grange, Tennessee, joined by the boys from the 2nd Iowa regiment.

We tore up the South for seventeen days and marched over eight hundred miles, destroying two railroads in the process. Just as Grant had figured, the chaos we created drew the Confederate defenders away from Vicksburg, and thus away from both Grant and Sherman's attack.

That's where my small group of scouts came in. It seems that almost everyone expected that after we hit Newton Station, we would turn back and return the same way we came in. Our colonel, however, reasoned that the Rebs would figure it that way as well, and he did just the opposite of what everyone expected. Since it was just as far down to the Union line in the south as it was back to La Grange, Tennessee, Colonel Grierson ordered us to keep riding south, right on down to Baton Rouge.

We rode over hundreds of miles that no Yankee unit had traveled before, often making fifty to seventy-five miles a day. At one point, just after Newton Station, a stray Confederate brigade picked up our tracks and almost rode right up our tail. Fortunately one of the scouts in our unit, an old coot nicknamed The Parson, knew of a route through some of the nastiest swamps I'd ever seen. He used to preach around the area before the war and had some experience with the Underground Railway, helping runaway slaves escape.

The Parson, Sergeant Hackworth, myself, and a man from the 7th named Ed Preston somehow found a way through all that muck and successfully brought the troop through the swamp. At very least we'd bought ourselves an extra day before those Rebels could even try to catch up with us.

When we finally came out of the swamp and back onto dry ground, Colonel Grierson ordered us to reconnoiter in order to find a quicker path to the Union lines down around Baton Rouge. After two hours, things were going well and we were about to turn back and report when we were jumped by a group of twenty or so locals.

We quickly dismounted and a fire fight broke

out. After their first volley Preston returned fire and shot a Rebel who was hiding behind a stump. Then they rushed us. The sergeant caught the rifle barrel of one of the attackers just behind the bayonet and spun him down and around. The man fell hard and in doing so let loose of his musket. The sergeant then pivoted in a circle so that the next Rebel ran right into that bayonet.

I was a mite occupied myself, struggling with a big soldier who had knocked me flat on my back. Off to the side I caught a glimpse of The Parson shooting another Rebel with his Colt percussion-cap pistol. As the big Rebel tried to choke me, I remembered a simple trick that Sarge had taught me, and I reached up under his grip and pinched the hell out of the skin on the side of his ribs. The man screamed and let go, giving me just enough time to pull my knife out and run him through.

I looked up and saw Sergeant Hackworth being grabbed on either side by two soldiers. He twisted a little, reversed their grip on his wrists, stepped back, and somehow or another spun their arms so the two men actually flipped forward, head over heels in the air, and landed hard on their backs. Both at the very same time! I swear I'd never seen anything like it in my life. He quickly pulled his revolver and between his shots, with some help from Ed Preston, the rest were dispatched in a hurry. Or at least so we thought.

I brushed myself off, and while everyone was recovering their mounts, I noticed that the first Rebel, the one who had lost his rifle when he was knocked to the ground had gotten up and was lifting up another rifle. He lined up to fire from a kneeling position. There was hardly any time to react.

"Hackworth, look out!" I yelled as I flung myself sideways across the sergeant's body. That's when I took the ball to the head. After he killed that man, the sergeant cradled me in his arms and washed the wound. "I owe you one, son," he said gently. "From here on out, anything you need, anytime, any place, you just call, and I'll come a-running." That's when I passed out.

I traveled the rest of the way to Baton Rouge on a makeshift travois, pulled by Hackworth's horse. Fortunately I've always had a hard head. Eventually we made it safely through, and during the whole campaign, much to the colonel's credit, we only had three killed, seven wounded, nine missing, and five men who we were forced to leave behind. From what they tell me it was one of Grant's finest moments during the whole war.

The raid also made a hero of Grierson although every man in the outfit already considered him one. There was not a single trooper in the brigade who wouldn't have ridden into hell for that man. On second thought, maybe that's just what we did. When we finally arrived at Baton Rouge, the colonel rode into town at the head of his column, sitting ramrod straight. As for the rest of us, we were so tired most of the men in the outfit arrived riding sound asleep in the saddle.

When the war ended, Sergeant Hackworth decided to retire, and that's when I told him about my ranch. Or at least about the land I owned and how I was hoping to start one. I offered him a full partnership but he declined. "I've had enough responsibility in my life," he explained. "How's about I just help ya maintain the place and keep ya company?"

I agreed, and we'd been together ever since.

Chapter Fourteen

The old soldier looked none the worse for wear since the last time I saw him, which was several months ago. Lobo tried to jump up on him, but the sergeant just pushed him away with his knee.

"Get off of me. Go on, get out of here," he chided. "Go play somewhere else, Lobo, some-where out of sight. Take your fleas with ya."

"Bad mood today?" I asked.

"Never did like strangers hanging around much," Sarge said.

"Strangers? What . . . here?"

Just then the door to the main house opened and

Lobo let out a short growl. A soldier walked out. I noticed he wore corporal's stripes on a cavalry uniform—an active duty uniform.

"What's he doing here?" I asked.

"Been eating us out of house and home until you returned," Sarge explained. "Going on three days now"—he looked over at the corporal—"and he's already been through half our food stock."

I chuckled. Admittedly the soldier was a little more ample around the girth than most men were back when I served. "What's he want?" I asked again.

The sergeant shrugged. "Says he has a message for you."

"So why didn't he just leave it with you?"

I guess the corporal got tired of being referred to as if he wasn't there. "I have instructions to deliver this letter to Corporal Kershaw personally and await a response before returning to the fort," he said.

"I ain't a corporal no more," I replied.

"Yes, sir," he answered.

"And don't 'sir' me. I work for a living."

"No, sir . . . er . . . I mean . . . no . . . er . . . ," he stammered.

Sarge just chuckled. "It's all right, sonny, just hand him the damn' letter," he ordered.

"Yes . . . ,"—Hackworth shot him a dirty look—"Sergeant."

"Close enough," he replied snidely. Then the

96

corporal, whose name I later learned was Alec Daniels, pulled a folded envelope from his tunic pocket and handed it to me.

I opened the letter and read it through twice, just to make sure. "No way," I growled. "No damned way! I just got back."

"What is it, Badger?" Hackworth asked. Concern showed on his face.

"It's from Fort Russell," I said, handing him the letter. "They need me to track someone down."

Sarge frowned. "What with all the men they got in uniform, the Army can't find a scout?"

"Maybe I can help with that," the corporal offered.

I sighed deeply. "All right, but let's go inside first. We got any rotgut left or did he drink that, too?"

The sergeant motioned to both of us. "Not the good stuff, he didn't."

I chuckled and turned to the dog, now sniffing around the leg of a decidedly uncomfortable corporal.

"Lobo, go hunt!" I commanded. The dog seemed to consider it for a moment, and then took off at a run.

We all turned and went indoors.

Once we were seated around the kitchen table, I took off my hat and hung it on the back of the chair. Sarge poured out three shots from a bottle of Irish whiskey he'd kept hidden. The letter was now unfolded on the table in front of us. I picked it up and re-read it.

I passed it to Sarge who also re-read it. "Not very specific, is it?" he remarked. "Just sort of says we need ya, so drop everything and come a-running."

The corporal nodded. "That's about it. The major was real insistent, too. Seems the higher-ups ordered him to find you. They asked specifically for you."

"Kinda strange, Badger, don't ya think?" Sarge remarked. "You rack up any big debts afore ya left the Army?"

I poured myself another shot and swallowed it in one gulp. "None that I remember." I looked over at the corporal. "So, Alec, what the hell's so important that an ex-scout's gotta earn more saddle sores?"

Sarge nodded. "Wondering that myself. They getting soft since I left?"

The corporal took a drink and shook his head. "Not hardly. I don't rightly understand it all myself. I wasn't able to gin up much about all this before they put me on a horse and slapped its rump," he said. "But it seems a Union Pacific train on its way West was robbed by some outlaw gang. The robbers attacked when the train stopped at a watering station. As I heard it told, the train was carrying a lot of people who were mostly heading to the fort. Some was robbed and some was kidnapped. Don't rightly know if there's been a ransom request or not. That's it. It's about all I know."

I put the letter back down on the table. "Corporal, thanks for coming all this way, but you'll have to go back empty-handed. I just got back from being too long out on the trail and don't rightly feel like doing anything besides kicking back and smoking a cigar. Besides, there doesn't seem to be any reason the Army can't handle this themselves." Shaking my head, I added: "Tell them I'm sorry, but rescuing rich bankers and whiskey peddlers just ain't particularly attractive to me right at the moment."

Corporal Daniels sighed, and then acted like he had suddenly remembered something important. "There was one other thing." He held up his glass hopefully, so I poured him another shot of whiskey.

"And just what might that be?" I asked.

"The major told me that if you gave me a hard time to mention specifically that it was women-folk that were taken."

"Damn," I muttered.

Sarge looked over at me and shrugged. "Women, huh? Well, don't nobody know the whole Dakota Territory better'n you do, Badger."

"Yeah, but I'm bushed," I replied truthfully. "Hell, fact is I'm half done in."

"So take the other half and ride out to the fort,"

Sarge replied. He took another drink. "Give them some helpful advice, and then come right back. Just because they send you a letter don't mean you're obligated to go riding all over the place. Remember, you ain't no Army scout no more. You're a civilian now. They can't give you no orders."

"I don't know, Sarge," I replied wearily. I looked over at the corporal. "Women, huh?"

"Yep, and one of them is the niece of some big colonel. Seems like he's the one who cabled the major to . . . and I quote . . . 'Go get the Badger!'"

I groaned and looked over at Sarge. We both answered out loud at the same time. "Grierson!"

The corporal smiled. "Yeah, that's the name. Know him?"

Sarge simply nodded. "What was it we used to say, Badger?"

I took another shot. It burned my throat. "That we'd march right down to hell and back for the man."

"Badger, looks like it's time to put up or shut up."

I groaned again and muttered: "Damn. All right, all right. I'll go."

Sarge looked over at the corporal. "We'll let the stock graze overnight and you can leave first thing in the morning."

"Yeah, I'll need them fresh for this one," I

agreed. "One night more won't change much, I guess."

Sarge shook his head. "Great, now I gotta feed this yahoo another dinner."

"Mind if I ask you something?" the corporal asked me.

"What?" I wondered.

"Why do they call you the Badger?"

I glared at him angrily and stuck my chin out with fire in my eyes. " 'Cause when I'm badgered into something I don't want to do, I get a real nasty disposition."

The corporal gulped. "Yes, sir, I don't doubt that."

I snapped back at him. "And don't call me 'sir'!"

Chapter Fifteen

Over dinner Sergeant Hackworth entertained us with tales of his time in the Far East. Alec Daniels was practically mesmerized by the stories. I'd learned long ago not to be surprised by anything the sergeant related. That man had proved to me long ago that he could back up just about anything he said.

I dropped another ladle full of pork and beans onto the corporal's plate. I believe it was his third. Sarge started telling him about a trip he had once taken to the countryside in Japan.

"The place isn't like anything you've ever experienced. The people have this sort of caste system with peasants, warlords, and a special warrior class they call samurai. You gotta see these fellows. They all carry two swords in their belts. They call the pair their *daisho*, which I learned refers to a long sword called a *katana* and a shorter one called a *wakizashi*. These samurai warriors carry their swords like we carry pistols, but, don't be fooled. They can carve you into little pieces quicker than you can blink."

Corporal Daniels was unimpressed. "No one is that fast. Especially not with a saber."

Sergeant Hackworth took a drink and continued: "Don't confuse the *katana* with no cavalry saber. Hell, those Army ones make better machetes than they do fighting weapons. The *katana* on the other hand ain't as curved, don't have as big a handle, and the point is more like a chisel than a pick. The damn' thing is sharp enough to shave with."

Alec chided him a mite. "But really faster than you can blink?"

Sarge nodded at us. "Let me put it this way. I once saw two of these samurai fellows square off at each other. Imagine two men from around here ready to draw on each other in the middle of the street, except these two were practically face to face."

My curiosity was piqued. I hadn't heard this story. "So what happened?"

"One of the men drew his sword and brought it up over his head in a looping movement intending to cut the other fellow."

"And?" Corporal Daniels prompted.

"Well, I wouldn't be lying if I told you I was almost positive he would win because the other samurai's sword warn't even out of its scabbard yet. But then the second samurai drew his sword and severed the first one's head clear off his body. All that on the draw, no less."

"What do you mean on the draw?" I asked, puzzled.

"He didn't even bring that sword around. He just cut the other man on the upswing while drawing the sword out from his belt. And I'll tell you he had that *katana*, sharp as it was, back in its scabbard without even looking at it. The dead samurai actually stood there for a second without his head before falling down. If the whole fight took more than a few seconds, I'll eat my hat."

"Damn," Alec said, letting out a gasp.

"Tell him about how you learned all that foot fighting stuff," I urged.

Sarge took another swig and wiped his mouth on his sleeve. "Well, at first those Jappers kept us pretty bottled up in the embassy. I guess they didn't want us foreign devils mingling with the locals. The warlord in those parts had our embassy completely surrounded by these samurai. At any rate, what with our being all cooped up, we were all pretty bored, so to pass the time we started learning their lingo with the help of a *geisha* they'd assigned us."

"*Geisha*?" Corporal Daniels asked.

"Sort of a high-classed, educated servant girl," Sarge explained. "Although I suspect they serve other purposes for the high muckety-mucks. Anyhow, I always had a knack for learning other folks' lingo. And like I said, we had a lot of time on our hands, so I picked it up pretty quick."

"You should hear him speak Comanche," I added.

"Don't change the subject," the sergeant said, taking another swig. "I'll lose my place."

"Sorry, go on," I said. "And pass that bottle."

"All right. So there I was, bored and protecting the embassy from a group of people who wanted very little to do with us. We were surrounded by samurai guards who were just as bored and just as curious. It made sense to break the monotony, so I just started talking to the guards."

"How'd they react to that?" Alec asked.

"Well, I'll tell you," Sarge replied, laughing. "The first time I walked up to one and asked if the rain would hurt the rhubarb, he almost passed out. To them I guess it was as if your mule suddenly said howdy. Once they got over their surprise, we sort of became friends. The ambassador started making inroads with their government officials, so we later got to move around more."

"Badger mentioned something about foot fighting?" Alec said.

"Right. Well, anyway, by that time we realized Ambassador Harris warn't in much danger, so he let me take up an invite by the samurai to train with them. Some of these fellows told me they actually guarded the Emperor once when he traveled through their protectorate. I'm telling you, these men were downright dangerous."

"Like you ain't?" I said sincerely. I had seen in action precisely what Sergeant Hackworth was capable of.

"I thought so, too, Badger, but truth is back then I was a babe in arms compared to those fellows. We set up a sparring match with one of the men I considered a friend. He was a skinny runt, so I felt pretty confident I warn't gonna make no fool of myself."

"What happened?" Alec asked, glued to his seat.

"I started off by throwing a left jab followed quickly by a right haymaker. I had a lot of boxing experience and was good enough to take most folks' heads off. Most folks except this one, that is. I got to tell you boys that little samurai deflected my punches like they were twigs and hit me in the elbow so hard my right arm went numb. He then stepped in and tripped me somehow, and the next thing I know I'm flat on my back.

"When I got back up, another samurai stepped

in and gave me the come-on sign. Not ganging up on me, mind ya, just practicing. Well, I dusted off my pride and went to tackle this fellow."

"I can see this one coming. You already taught me this one," I guessed.

"Yep. Quicker than you know, he flips me over his hip, and there I am right on my back again. Now I'm pissed, so I stood up, brought my dukes up again, and gave the next one the same come-and-get-it gesture."

I chuckled because I could imagine what was coming.

The sergeant continued: "So I made sure my stance was right and flexed my arms, and then the man kicked me in the head. So help me he was facing me less than a foot or so away when he kicked me on the right side of my face with his right foot. Think about it, the right side of my face with his right foot. The kick was some sort of outside-inward dipsy-doodle. Hell, I don't think he even raised his hand."

"Did you get in any good ones?" Alec asked.

"Good ones?" Sarge replied. "I never laid a hand on any of them. That kick put me down like a rock. After that I spent as much time as I could getting my ass kicked until I learned to do it as good as they could."

"Maybe even a little better," I observed.

The sergeant grinned. "Maybe."

Chapter Sixteen

The following morning I was again astride my Appaloosa with the mule tied behind. His kack had been restocked with supplies, but I left the chestnut mare behind in the corral. She would serve nicely later as breeding stock for our small but growing herd.

"I should be going with you on this one, Badger," Sarge commented.

"I need you here to run the place," I remarked truthfully. "Besides, I like what you've done with the broken door latch. And it only took you two months."

"Very funny. Seriously, this one could get messy."

"All I intend to do is ride to the fort and give them some advice, just like you suggested, Sarge."

"Sure," he replied. It sounded to me like he didn't believe that for one minute.

"All right, Alec," I said to the soldier to my left. "Let's move it out."

Lobo had returned to the house sometime during the night and at the moment was occupied with a rather large bone. What was left of it looked to me like it might have been from a large ram or elk. I whistled, pointed out the gate, and we took off at a lope.

"Big dog," the corporal commented after a while. "Or is he a wolf?"

"A little of both," I said as we rode on.

"You sure he won't bite me?" he asked nervously.

"Nah, he won't bite ya," I said. Alec looked relieved. "He'll just swallow you whole."

The soldier shook his head. "Very funny, but I don't doubt it for a moment."

"He's a pretty good judge of character," I advised. "Just don't make any fast moves toward me and he'll leave you alone. Oh, and remember that whatever you do, don't say the word G-U-N, out loud," I added.

"And that would be because?" the corporal asked.

"When he was a puppy, or cub if you prefer, I taught him to attack on command. G-U-N is the attack command. Unless you want to end up as his lunch, I'd avoid the word when he's around."

Corporal Daniels gulped. "Really? And just how'd you teach him that?"

"Well, over the years I've learned that dogs prefer consistency and repetition. Hell, if you don't train them, they'll end up training you."

"Guess so. Makes sense, now that you mention it."

"So you do your training regularly and always the same way. Make it fun and they catch on quick," I said.

"That's all?"

"'Course not. You also got to take advantage of their natural behavior."

"In what way?" he asked.

"Well, for instance, if a puppy sits down on his own, you say . . . 'Sit.' Similarly if he runs to you all by his lonesome, you say . . . 'Come.' He begins to associate the word with the action. Then you begin putting him on a rope and pull while saying . . . 'Come.' Then you reward him for performing the action with a piece of chicken or something. Dog doesn't come, he doesn't get a reward. He'll get the idea right quick."

"Purty clever, I'd say."

I shook my head. "Just common sense."

"So what about the attack word? How'd you do that?"

I thought my answer over for a moment. "Well, there's some folks what believe in hitting and hollering at pups all the time, but I don't cotton to that way of training."

"No?"

I shook my head. "Nope, I don't beat on my animals. No need if ya know what you're doing. I started out with Lobo by playing tug of war with ropes or whatever sticks he fancied. Then I moved up to things like ham hocks. Or I'd get a big branch and wrap it in burlap so it looked like an arm and tie the end to a you-know-what." I made a pistol gesture with my hand.

"Oh I get it. So he thinks it's play when he's biting on things. That's how he learns to hang on when you pull back, right?"

"Right. I even had Sarge running around with his arm wrapped in layers of cotton and burlap sacks. Lobo bit so hard, Sarge couldn't lift a coffee mug for a week with his right arm. Even after wearing all that padding."

I looked down at Lobo and pointed. "Go hunt." The big animal took off at a lope and was quickly out of sight.

"Don't you worry he'll lose us, or vice-versa?"

I shook my head. "Was at first, but he's never failed to return yet. Has a really powerful sense of smell, I guess. Or maybe it's some sort of wolf instinct. He may be gone for days on end, but he always returns. Every time."

"Remarkable," the corporal said.

"I don't know." I smiled. "Maybe he just gets lonely for the horse."

We rode on for a while before Corporal Daniels piped up again. "So, you and the Sarge go back a ways?"

I looked over at him. "You ask too many questions, Alec." Maybe it was a little harsh since it was obvious the corporal meant no harm. It's just that I was used to riding alone and liked to keep my eyes and ears open while on the trail, especially in the Territory. You stay alive that way. Surest way to get bushwhacked is to jabber away all the time, instead of paying attention to detail.

The soldier looked dejected and after a short time I felt a mite guilty. "Look, Corporal, it's just that for most of my life I've ridden solo. I've kept my scalp by listening more than palavering. Hell, even when I was in the Army, I usually rode point instead of hanging back with the troop."

"Makes sense. But Injuns don't hardly give us any problems any more. Not since the Custer slaughter. Ain't many of them around these parts that act up much."

I sighed. "So who robbed the train? Who kidnapped them folks?"

Corporal Daniels looked over at me. "Oh, I see what you mean."

I didn't see myself as this boy's teacher, but the corporal needed some schooling. I remembered that I hadn't been born trail-wise, either. Oh, sure, I'd learned some in my early years, but during the war the Sarge had helped further educate me to the way of things.

"Give ya an example," I offered. "What sort of possible . . . let's say, worrisome things . . . have you noticed in the last three hours?"

"Not much," he replied. "We missed a couple of prairie dog holes the horses might have stepped in, I guess."

I shook my head in disbelief. "So soon after the war and it's a wonder the Army can still march a mile without shooting itself in the foot." I reined the Appaloosa and came to a stop.

"All right, look around. Concentrate. What do you see?" I asked.

The corporal took his time. "Nothing to worry me." He shrugged his shoulders. "Sorry."

My eyes rolled up. "See that tree over there? See the grizzly fur on it from where it rubbed. Might come back on us if it's hungry enough. Or how about over there . . . down to your right." I pointed. "See the hole? Might be a rattlesnake somewhere near. Hell, at a distance I'm blind as a bat but even I can see sun reflections. There's something shiny over on the hill there, off to the left."

"Damn. I never noticed that," Corporal Daniels said, shaking his head in disbelief. "Wait, there's that reflection again. I see what you're talking about now."

I took out my scope and looked up at the bluff.

"Trouble?" the corporal asked anxiously.

I took my time before answering. "Doesn't appear to be. Looks like a couple of prospectors or maybe trappers trailing a couple of pack mules."

The corporal relaxed. "So we're all right."

I looked at him. "That's precisely my point. We're never all right. Leastwise I ain't. Not until I'm home, that is."

The soldier nodded. "I get ya now. Sorry."

"Don't apologize so much. Sarge says it's a sign of weakness."

I nudged the Appaloosa and we rode on. It couldn't have been five minutes before Alec opened up again.

"Mind if I ask you something?"

I dropped my head in exasperation. He would never learn. "What now?" I growled.

"Well, I was wondering. I heard tell you was a bounty kill- . . . um . . . a bounty hunter."

"And?"

"Well, I was just wondering if it's true, and, if so, why you do it. I mean after seeing your ranch, it seems to me if I had a nice spread like that I'd want to stay on it. No offense meant."

"That so?" I asked, annoyed.

"Well?"

I considered my reply. "Look, Alec, I really don't have a full answer for you. Something keeps drawing me back. Something seems . . ."—I searched for the right word—"unsettled. I go back to working the ranch with Sarge, but in spite of how great it feels to build something with my own hands, sooner or later something or someone comes along and off I go."

"Don't it bother ya to kill a man like that?" he asked.

Frustrated, I looked over at him. "With the exception I'm about to make with a snot-nosed corporal, I never did in a man who wasn't guilty of a major crime and never without giving him a chance to surrender."

113

" 'Nuff said," the corporal replied timidly. "Still, all and all it's a tough way to live."

"Oh, and riding in the cavalry is a walk in the park with a bouquet of roses. Remember, I've been there and done it."

"Right. Got it."

It took us five days of hard riding to get to Fort David A. Russell. My ears were ringing from all the noise I had to endure the whole way there.

Chapter Seventeen

The fort was located just outside of Cheyenne. It was named after the General David Allen Russell who was killed at the Battle of Opequon during the Civil War. Units of the 30th Infantry under Colonel John D. Stevenson started work on the fort around 1867 in order to protect workers of the Union Pacific Railroad. In September of that year Company H of the 2nd Cavalry rode in formally to establish the fort and to take charge.

Fort D.A. Russell didn't have the large stockade gates you usually found on Army forts in the West because there had been no hostile activities from the local tribes at the time it had been built. With its usual effectiveness the government decided to build the most impressive fort they could with the cheapest materials and the most

114

economic labor. That meant using its own soldiers as craftsmen for the tidy sum of 35¢ a day.

Some of the buildings for the fort were even prefabricated in Chicago and then shipped in. The majority of the structures were made of planed boards and battens, which is a mud mixture used to fill in the cracks. I had it on good authority the barracks were still drafty in the fall and more often than not in winter were colder than a general's heart.

The officers' quarters were usually about a story and a half and were built as doubles. They averaged about five rooms to a unit. Inside there would be a parlor, dining room, and kitchen on the first floor and two bedrooms on the second.

Corporal Daniels and I rode across the rather large drill field and over to the post's livery stable. Once we'd put up our horses, the corporal accompanied me over to the major's office.

"I appreciate your help, Alec, but I can handle it from here," I said gratefully.

"If you decide to go after those robbers and need help, I'd like to ride with you," he offered eagerly.

I shook my head. "You've been in the Army long enough to know never to volunteer for anything. Besides, I work alone. No offense. You know how it is."

"None taken."

"And, Alec," I added, "I'd appreciate it if you'd keep an eye on Lobo while we're still here.

He tends to attract trouble like honey does a fly."

"No problem," Corporal Daniels replied. "We've become surprisingly good friends."

"So I noticed. But be careful, anyway. Anything happens . . . remember, I told ya so."

"You watch your back . . . Badger," he said somewhat apprehensively, as if using my nickname was taking too much for granted.

"You, too, Corporal. I'll look for you later this evening." I threw him a sloppy salute, turned, and entered the major's office.

Inside, there was an orderly sitting at a rather small desk facing the major's door. Or perhaps the orderly was too big for the desk. I began to wonder if the physical standards for the whole Army had been altered.

"May I help you?" the orderly asked.

"I'm here to see the major," I replied. I handed him my letter. "I'm here at his request."

The orderly, a staff sergeant, glanced at the letter. "Please wait a moment while I let him know you're here."

"No problem."

The orderly disappeared for a few moments, giving me time to look around the anteroom. There was not much in it to attract attention except for a framed newspaper article hanging on the far wall. I stepped closer and started to read.

St. Charles *Daily Gazette*
August 29th 1864
St. Charles, Illinois

One of our local citizens has been cited for bravery for his actions during the Peninsular campaign with the 8th Illinois Cavalry. As our readers are aware, the 8th Illinois was mustered into the Army of the Potomac in September, 1861 under the command of Colonel John F. Farnsworth. After their first major battle at Williamsburg the 8th cavalry were constantly in the advance vanguard of the Union Army.

On June 26th, 1861 six companies of the 8th Illinois Cavalry met the advance of the Rebel Army under the now famous Confederate General Thomas Jonathan "Stonewall" Jackson at Mechanicsville, Virginia. The gallant Illinois troopers held the line from the early morning until 3 o'clock in the afternoon, at which time they were ordered to retire.

During this action a young Captain Fred Parks was leading his men on horseback when he noticed a group of Union soldiers retreating from a Rebel charge. Captain Parks realized that their line of retreat led across a narrow stone bridge that was in immediate danger of being overrun by enemy troops. In spite of orders to the contrary Captain Parks ordered his men to dismount, to advance, and to protect the bridge.

At this point during this engagement Captain Parks's men ran toward a shallow ravine at the base of the bridge. A Union ambulance was next seen galloping toward the bridge under enemy fire. The volleys from Rebel sharpshooters on the other side were intense and several of the captain's brave troopers fell dead.

Apparently a few Union soldiers next started to retreat when Captain Parks, in complete disregard for his own personal safety, suddenly stood up and drew his saber. Sticking his sword through the crown of his hat and waving it aloft as a signal to his men, he was heard to shout: "We can't abandon our own men. Follow me, boys! Onward! Let's protect that ambulance!"

Encouraged by their leader and inspired by his gallantry, the Union men charged, retook the bridge, and saved the ambulance from destruction. Colonel Farnsworth later rode up with his entourage and, after listening to a brief explanation of the circumstances, noticed that Captain Parks had been wounded in the shoulder.

The colonel quickly ordered that the captain be removed to the rear of the Federal lines where prompt medical attention was rendered.

On the 5th of August of 1864 Captain Fred Parks was awarded the Army's highest commendation, the Medal of Honor. This commendation is now the nation's highest medal for valor in combat that can be awarded to members of the armed forces. The medal was first authorized in 1861 for Navy personnel and Marines, and the following year for Army soldiers as well.

Present at the ceremony were the captain's family and the presiding officer, General Alfred Pleasonton. In addition, the mayor of St. Charles, Illinois and the editor of this *Gazette* were in attendance. The town of St. Charles is most proud to be Captain Parks's home town.

There was no doubt in my mind that the major would be a most impressive man. By now everyone knows that particular medal is not given out lightly.

"Enter," a voice ordered.

The sergeant opened the door for me and I walked into the major's office.

"I'm Kershaw, Major. You sent for me?"

There was a small carved wooden name plate

on the desk that read simply: MAJOR FRED PARKS.

The major rose and extended a hand in greeting. He was tall, firmly built, and stood erect, as if he had a board strapped to his backside. The major had a fair amount of hair for a man of his age but it was graying around the edges. His handshake was firm and I suspect was a little stronger than usual, probably offered in an attempt to size men up in a hurry.

"Don't judge by the grip, Major. I've had a problem with my right side since childhood. Learned to deal with it a long time ago, though. Got through the war with it all right."

"So they tell me," he replied. "Have a seat." He indicated one of the two chairs located in front of his desk. Returning to his side of his desk, he sat down and arranged some paperwork. I suspect this was either a stall to impress me or perhaps was simply a means of creating enough time to gather his thoughts.

The major cleared his throat and looked up at me. "Let me make this brief. A little over a week ago a train was robbed out in the territory, northeast of here. A gang of about fifteen men attacked the train with military precision. They hog-tied the engineers when the train stopped at a water tower and robbed the passengers. They also killed two men who tried to resist and made off with the payroll. To make matters worse there were several young ladies on board and they made off with them."

"Hostages?" I asked.

"We don't know," he replied, shaking his head. "There hasn't been a ransom request and our patrols haven't recovered any bodies."

"Do you know how many women were taken exactly?"

"Four," he replied sadly.

At that point there was another knock on the door.

"Proceed," Major Parks said firmly.

A captain in his mid-thirties entered and saluted. Looking me over, he addressed the major. "This him, sir? Is this the tracker?"

"Yes, I am," I answered before the major could reply. I never did like being spoken about as if I weren't even in the room.

"Well, are you going after them or not? If so, I want in," the captain informed me.

"Whoa, hang on a second," I said, raising my voice. "I haven't agreed to anything yet. I still haven't even heard all the particulars."

The captain looked frustrated and the major annoyed.

"We've had this discussion before, Captain Boyle," the major replied sternly. "The new Posse Comitatus Act specifically prohibits military personnel from acting in a law enforcement capacity while on U.S. soil."

"What?" I asked, confused. "Whose posse is that? What do you need me for if you already have a posse out there?"

The major shook his head and held up a hand. "Bear with me a minute. I'm sorry for the misunderstanding but Posse Comitatus is the name of a new act passed by Congress. I have it around here somewhere." He shuffled some papers on his desk while Captain Boyle paced nervously.

"Here it is," he said, picking up one of the papers. "Let me read . . . 'Whoever, except in cases and under circumstances expressly authorized by the Constitution or Act of Congress, willfully uses any part of the Army as a posse comitatus or otherwise to execute the laws shall be fined under this title or imprisoned not more than two years.' " Major Parks paused a moment to consider his words. "From what they tell me it was some sort of political deal agreed upon in exchange for electoral votes in the last election. Pass this act and the government will withdraw troops from the South. Tit for tat," he explained.

"I get it. Damned politicians again. Now the Army can't even act," I said, shaking my head. "So, why not just let the proper authorities handle it?"

"A lot of good that'll do," Boyle replied angrily.

"Calm down, Captain," the major snapped. "I understand your concerns but calm down, anyway. Mister Kershaw," he said, addressing me directly, "several of the officers on this post have a personal interest in seeing this resolved successfully. You see, three of them are engaged to women from the train and at least two other soldiers are related to them." The major paused before adding: "Not to mention the payroll our enlisted men were counting on." He quickly held up a hand, the gesture clearly meant for the captain. "And before you say anything that you'll regret, please realize that I do not mean to imply for a moment that the money is anywhere near as important as getting those ladies back." Then he addressed me again directly. "That is where you come in."

I shook my head. "Actually, I was sort of expecting merely to offer some advice or maybe help with directions to the Army, and then get back home. This sort of thing could take quite a while and might not have an outcome all that good. Again, why not just let the local authorities handle it?"

"Out of the question," the major declared. "We don't have a lot of time. Not with women involved." He shook his head. "Also the territorial marshal in charge of this area recently took a fall from his horse and broke his neck. Apparently a rattler startled his horse and bucked him off. Died right there where he fell. Furthermore, most of the local town's lawmen are claiming they've got no jurisdiction." He paused to consider his words. "Look, I don't know a lot about you, Mister Kershaw, but I trust Colonel Benjamin Grierson implicitly. When I cabled him about his niece, his immediate response was to instruct me to send for you. Apparently he has the same sort of trust and confidence in you that I have in him."

"I'd do anything for the colonel, too. But a gang of fifteen men or more . . . I don't know about this."

Captain Boyle spoke up, addressing Major Parks and seemingly ignoring me. "Sir, there are several of us willing to go undercover to help this man. If necessary, we'll resign our commissions."

"That won't be necessary," I said before the major had a chance to reply. "If I decide to do this job, I'll do it alone."

The captain became agitated. "Against a large, well-armed gang of hardcases? I think not," he said angrily.

"I can only imagine how worried you are, Captain, but I have my reasons."

"And those might be?" Major Parks asked, leaning back slightly in his chair.

I considered my answer carefully. "First of all, I don't want someone so emotionally attached coming with me on this. Anger and worry clouds your judgment too much and that might get me killed. I don't cotton much to me getting killed."

"Can't fault you there," said the major. "What else?"

I waited for a moment before explaining further. I was sure it would be a sore spot. "Then there's all that cavalry training. You go charging in there with sabers flashing and likely as not they will kill the hostages."

The major cleared his throat while Captain Boyle glared at me. "Go on," the major said calmly.

"I know how I work, but don't know anything about the captain. The last thing I need is someone unfamiliar with this sort of work getting in my way."

"I am a career Army officer," the captain protested.

"Right, and the last time I checked the cavalry doesn't do much of a job teaching things like stalking silently on foot, reading sign, fitting in with outlaws, and, if necessary, killing someone with your bare hands. Where I'm going, we won't be doing any saluting or parade drills. No offense."

"But I understood you were in the Army once," the major offered.

"Yes, sir, I was, and I learned a lot. But not about bounty hunting. That I picked up on my own over the years."

The captain rolled his eyes. "Great, a professional bounty killer."

"Don't like that term, Captain. If it's all the same with you, I prefer the term bounty man, or if you prefer bounty hunter. I don't kill for the bounty. I only kill as a last resort and only in self-defense. You want some Goody Two Shoes to go after these killers, fine, but count me out. Oh, and if you do, I'd start by putting up a few head-stones ahead of time for them girls." I was hot under the collar and getting hotter by the minute.

"That'll be enough of that, Mister Kershaw. As I explained previously, if Colonel Grierson trusts you, well then, that's good enough for me." He turned to Captain Boyle. "And remember, Captain, the colonel is personally involved as much as any of us are. They took his niece, too, remember?"

"Sorry, sir," the rebuked captain replied.

"Look, Captain," I said, "this is a job for a whole troop or for one man. Trust me, anything else will end badly. And the major already explained why we can't use your troops." I turned to Major Parks. "I assume the railroad authorities are already working on this?"

The major nodded. "They covered the whole area as soon as they could, but so far they've come up empty-handed. It's as if the gang disappeared into thin air."

"More likely the outlaws know the territory better, already had an escape route planned, and covered their tracks well."

"So what do you aim to do that the rest can't?" the captain asked anxiously.

"First of all, I'm going to face facts. If there has

been no note or ransom by now, then I expect they didn't kidnap the women for profit. They'd surely know that there's more money to be made from family and friends than if they sold them as slaves."

Major Parks looked at Captain Boyle uncomfortably before asking the expected question. "So they would have killed them?"

I shook my head. "Not necessarily. More likely they are thinking along the lines of . . . shall we say, personal entertainment. Kinda lonely out in the territory."

"You bastard, that's my fiancée, Suzanne, you're talking about," muttered the captain.

"Makes sense, though," I explained, shrugging. "All this time and the local lawmen haven't found any bodies. No ransom demands. Gang of hardened killers. Only logical conclusion. You willing to accept that possibility?" I asked the captain.

Boyle stared at me, and then looked out the window for a while. "I don't care. I just want her back." He was almost moved to tears. That one response actually helped improve my opinion of him.

"So where does that get us?" the major interrupted.

"Every pursuit has a track of its own. We, or I should say I, start by crossing that track. Now, if it is a gang that big and they plan on keeping these women, then they have to have some place to keep them. The trick is to find that place."

"And how do you intend to do that?" Boyle asked.

"First I need to know if any of the people on the train are still around. Then I need to have a talk with them before I decide if I'll do this or not."

"We already interviewed them and came up with nothing," the major explained.

I shrugged my shoulders. "Depends on the questions and on who's doing the asking. Sometimes witnesses exaggerate, sometimes they are still afraid or timid, and sometimes they simply won't say anything to an authority figure in uniform. Occasionally you got to read between the lines."

"And what about supplies?" Major Parks asked.

"I pack my own, but I would appreciate a place to stay tonight while I talk to the survivors. I'm not promising anything, mind you, but, if I do decide to go, I'll be leaving in the morning."

The captain looked at me and frowned. "And I suppose you'll be negotiating the price first?"

"That's uncalled for Boyle," the major cautioned.

"But a fair enough question, Major," I agreed angrily. "Normally I would be . . . what'd you call it? . . . negotiating, but seeing as how it's for Colonel Grierson, I don't care." I got up to leave the room, but before I reached the door I turned to the captain. " 'Course, if there is any paper out on these men, I'll take whatever reward is thrown my way just to make you happy. Good enough, Captain?" I didn't wait to hear his reply and closed the door, hard, after me.

Chapter Eighteen

Just as the two officers had indicated, some of the people who had been robbed on the train were now at the fort. I spent the better part of the afternoon talking to as many as I could. As I could have predicted, much of what the witnesses had to offer was of little value.

"Many riders, big guns, evil eyes," were some of the vague and mostly worthless descriptions they gave. "One man was clean-shaven and wore two guns cross-draw style." Another heard someone call one of the leaders Hank. The number of riders varied according to one witness or another from "exactly fifteen" to "thirty or more."

A couple of people offered more specific information such as—"One had a big round Stetson with a studded hatband on it."—or "Another wore chaps with white leather stitching." All in all it was about as I expected, but often it's more about what is not said than what is. Over the years I'd learned to put multiple descriptions together and then sift out the silt. The leftovers could often be of value.

What I was eventually able to piece together was that there appeared to be two men in their late forties or early fifties who seemed to be in charge. The heavier of the two was the one who did the shooting, and that apparently had been touched off when a male passenger grabbed at the outlaw and tore off his bandanna. The overall attack seemed well co-ordinated, so it stood to reason that in all likelihood the gang had done this sort of thing before.

Nobody saw any pack animals, so I figured they must have ridden off with what they needed in their saddlebags. That, in turn, indicated to me that they didn't plan on riding very far without either restocking or holing up somewhere.

I knew they wouldn't head for a well-settled town, at least not with women prisoners in tow. No decent Western town would put up with that. No *decent* town . . . That got me thinking. For years there had been stories of a town without law. A town where the inhabitants were all on the lam. It was supposed to be a hell hole of a place where the rules were all reversed.

I also knew from experience that lawmen often spoke of a pass near Johnson County. Supposedly, going back to the early 1860s, no posse had ever successfully penetrated the pass when pursuing fugitives. Rumor had it there were various hide-outs or camps in the valleys on the other side where criminals took refuge and found safety in numbers. It made sense that if that outlaw town were anywhere to be found, it would be on the other side of Hole-in-the-Wall Pass, in the Bighorns.

I studied one of the fort's maps. It was not too much of a stretch to imagine riding from where the robbery occurred over to that pass in the mountains. I knew that local lawmen would comb all the other known hiding places. Whenever a woman was mishandled, the entire West would take up arms. One or more of the railroad posses would be combing the territory as well. If they hadn't found anything by now, then it stood to reason I'd have to do something different. Go where they wouldn't. Or couldn't.

I didn't like it, but it seemed there was only one course of action that made any sense to me. I had gathered all the information I could at the fort for now, so I decided I deserved a break. I walked over to the base's sutler store to get myself a drink.

Along the way I picked up Corporal Daniels and made sure my animals had been well cared for. I asked the base farrier to check the horse and mule for me and made sure Lobo was tied up safely near the Appaloosa. He looked too much like a wolf to be allowed to run loose around a military base full of armed and itchy recruits.

Once inside the store I ordered two beers and handed one to the corporal.

"Sure I can't go with you on this? Won't you change your mind and take me along?"

I shook my head and once again explained the reasons why. It was at that moment that a group of officers and non-coms entered the store and approached us. I counted a 1st and 2nd lieutenant, two sergeants, and a corporal. Any time I see a group purposely heading my way, I instinctively get worried. You never can predict what a mob will do and it doesn't always end up with a parade down Main Street with you held up on the crowd's shoulders. I switched the beer to my left hand while my right dropped slowly down to my holster.

"Can I help you boys?" I asked quietly.

The men shifted around for a moment as one of the sergeants reached into his pocket. He seemed to be sizing me up, which was understandable, but made no threatening gestures.

"Go ahead, Sergeant," the 1st lieutenant ordered.

"You the one they call the Badger?" he asked.

"That'll do." I nodded my head.

"The word is you are going out after the women what was took from the train. That true?"

I put the mug of beer down before answering. "Yep. It is now. I've decided to go. Leaving at first light."

He nodded and handed me the picture he'd

retrieved from his blouse pocket. "This here's my sister. Name's Eileen. Since our folks died, she's all I have in the world." He looked around. "Exceptin' fer these men, here. I need to know if you can do this. If you can fetch her back."

The 1st lieutenant added: "I am engaged to her, sir, and I want to make sure no harm comes to her. The other men here all have similar interests with the other women."

I nodded slowly. "Lieutenant, would it help to know I did a hitch with the Sixth Illinois before I got into this line of work. Got out a corporal."

The men all seemed to relax some. One of the other sergeants smiled. "Had a brother who served with the Seventh. You in on that big raid of Grierson's?"

I nodded back. "Rode point all the way. That's mostly why I'm doing this. Grierson got me back alive and I intend to do the same for his niece."

The 2nd lieutenant asked: "Pardon me, but you ever done anything like this before? Rescue work, I mean."

"Sort of." I was being truthful. "First you have to track and find them. No one better at that than I am, and that's a fact, not a boast. Then you have to size up the competition and figure out a plan. That's the hard part 'cause no two outlaws act the same. Going on fourteen years now and I'm still in one piece. A lot of bad men aren't. But the truth is once a man on the run is found, it all depends on circumstance and of course a lot of luck." I paused. "You asked, so I'm telling."

The men considered my remarks. "Is there anyway we can help?" the 1st lieutenant asked.

"Let me buy you a beer. I'll tell you my plan and you can make any suggestions you like." I cautioned: "Just so's ya know, I usually never discuss things like this. I'm making an exception 'cause it's your family and our Army, but, remember, one blabbermouth and it might get back to the ones I'm after. I don't much fancy letting the enemy know any of my moves."

"Makes sense," two agreed aloud.

"Anything else?" the 1st lieutenant asked.

I thought a minute. "Could use a good pair of Army binocs."

"The store sells a couple of good ones," the 2nd lieutenant told me. He turned to the store clerk. "Show this man the binoculars you have for sale. Let him pick any pair he wants and put it on my account."

"Much obliged," I replied. After throwing down a few more brews, I asked the sergeant for the picture he had shown me. "I know how much it means to you, but it just might help me get her back."

"In that case, gladly," the sergeant replied.

"Just sign your name on the back. First name only and nothing else."

"Sure, anything for Eileen. Like I said, she's all I got."

"Any other pictures would help," I mentioned.

The men gathered around and I unrolled a map. We discussed my idea for an hour or so, and tossed down a few more beers. Then the group thanked me and reluctantly returned to their duties.

Later that evening, I requested a final meeting with Major Parks to let him personally know I would accept the job and to discuss my plan with him. I also requested he inform Colonel Grierson by telegraph that his wishes were being fulfilled, but urged the major not to explain how. While I had no reason to doubt the honesty of most telegraphers, I felt there was no need to allow that sort of information to float around out there among all those loose wires. Better safe than sorry, especially when it comes to my own hide.

As far as I was concerned, whether Major Parks agreed with me or not was irrelevant. It was my own survival I was worried about. That, and carrying out my mission successfully in order to repay what I felt was, as simplistic as it may sound, a debt of honor to an old commander.

"There is one last favor you can do for me, Major," I said as our discussion was coming to an end.

"Anything within reason. What do you need?"

"Can you get the base to print me up a poster by morning?"

The major smiled. "If there was ever a complaint

about how I run things, it would be that I issue too many memorandums. We keep our printer busy here, no doubt about that. One more sheet of paper shouldn't matter much. What do you want it to say?"

I looked at him seriously. "I need a Wanted Dead or Alive poster printed with information about me on it. Say, for robbing a Wells, Fargo station and shooting the guard."

At first the major looked puzzled, but then quickly caught on. "You need proof to avoid suspicion amongst the outlaws."

I nodded. "Where I'm going the badder the better."

"I'll make sure you have what you need by morning," Major Parks said, extending a hand. "And good luck to you."

"I expect I'll need it. Thank you, Major." I got up and left the room.

I stayed overnight in the barracks and rechecked my supplies.

The following morning, just before I left Fort Russell, I met up with Corporal Daniels. As I mounted the Appaloosa, he handed me a canteen. I looked at him rather puzzled.

"Thanks, Alec, but I already have a canteen full of water and a big water bag on the mule. I'm good for now."

"I'm sure Sergeant Hackworth would want you to take this with ya," the corporal explained, smiling. "A little something from the Emerald Isle. Something to ease the aches and pains on the trail."

I unscrewed the cap and sniffed the canteen's contents. It almost made my nose run and my eyes water. "Must be about ninety-eight proof Irish . . . er . . . water."

"Just about," he answered with a chuckle. "Good luck, Badger. Wish I were going with you."

I looked out the gate and to the horizon and shook my head. "No you don't, Alec. Trust me, you don't."

Chapter Nineteen

I drew a line on the map from the watering station where the train robbery had taken place straight across to where the Hole-in-the-Wall Pass was supposed to be located. Then I drew a second line from Fort David A. Russell to a point on the map halfway across the first line. My intent was to ride to a place that would cross the gang's path about halfway. I wasn't counting on meeting the outlaws on the trail. I knew by now they would be too far gone for that ever to succeed. I did, however, want to come up right behind them in order to verify my suspicions.

The kidnappers would have ridden hard and straight toward what they perceived to be a safe haven. That would be especially important to them since they would be traveling with four unwilling women. Somewhere along that route I should be able to cut sign. Then I would know for sure if I was on the right track.

I had another reason for riding in this direction. If my calculations were correct, sooner or later I'd have to enter that same pass. I knew no one on the right side of the law had ever made it through there alive, so I had to have an edge, a hole card if you will.

By heading directly up the second line I'd drawn on the map, the one that took me north, I'd ride right through the town of Bighorn Gulch. I knew the place all too well, and believed I'd find someone there who could provide me with the necessary information I needed to help me get in and out of that pass alive and in one piece.

Just as I had calculated, three days of hard travel north brought me to Bighorn Gulch. It was one of those small towns that were springing up all over the territory. At the time I couldn't help but wonder if this one would eventually make it or not. Half tent and half wood, part corral and part shops, it seemed to me the town couldn't decide if it was going to mine or subsist on cattle.

Other than freight offices, a barbershop, and two general stores, Bighorn Gulch had one jail that was seldom occupied, three saloons, but no church. There was nothing particularly memorable about the place other than the fact that I knew it wasn't overly concerned with the moral fiber of its citizenry.

I'd met the town's sheriff a year or so ago when he was elected out of default. By that I mean no one else wanted the job. Besides, the mayor was his brother-in-law. I doubt that sheriff had ever drawn a gun in anger, let alone as part of his job. He spent more time sleeping in the jail's empty cells and drinking rotgut than anything else.

When the dime novels talk about a lawman striking fear into the hearts of outlaws, Bighorn Gulch's sheriff was clearly not the one they were referring to. This town was precisely the kind of place that I could count on to harbor someone with the know-how I needed to rescue those women.

I sat on the Appaloosa, staring down at Lobo. He'd been gone for a half day, and just before I reached Bighorn's town limits he had returned, as usual playfully barking and nipping at the horse's hoofs.

"Lobo, behave," I ordered, for all the good I knew it would do. The dog trotted behind the horse and mule till we came to a stop in front of one of the saloons. I dismounted, and tied the horse and mule to the hitching rail.

"Lobo, guard!" I didn't really have to worry much about him because over the years we had done this time and time again. Because Lobo got along great with the big gelding, he actually preferred staying near him. This time I insisted on it because I didn't want a repetition of the incident at the last saloon we'd been to.

I didn't give a hoot in hell about someone like that Wilkins fellow getting his leg bit, but I didn't want Lobo wandering around, creating his usual fear and havoc. I couldn't afford to lose any more time. Not now.

The big dog looked up at me, wagged his tail, and barked.

"I mean it, Lobo, stay! Guard the horse!" He may not have understood my words, but he always understood my meaning.

I checked the shells in my sidearm. I always carried a twelve-gauge buckshot load in the left chamber and a shotgun slug in the right. Once I was confident everything was as it should be, I re-holstered it. I took a deep breath and walked into the saloon.

When you are looking for the answer as to why the sky is blue, you need the schoolmarm, so you go to the nearest school. When you want to know how to do something illegal, you head for places where outlaws hang out. And that of course meant the nearest saloon. Besides, another mug of beer never hurt anyone.

When I entered the tavern, I immediately read the room. It's an old gambling term that refers to sizing up the competition. In this case I wanted to avoid anyone who might know me, or might hold a grudge, or get in my way. What I was looking for was a certain kind of person. The one I wanted would be right off a Wanted poster.

Ever since I can remember I've had a good memory for faces and years of perusing posters in sheriff's offices, banks, and post offices all over the West had sharpened that ability.

I approached the bar and ordered a beer. There was a side table at the end of the counter with a large side of cooked beef on a skewer. There were some small plates and a carving knife on the table next to the skewer. I tossed an extra coin on the bar and sliced a hunk of meat. Then I walked over to one of the tables and sat down, facing the entrance with my back to the wall. I pulled my hat down lower over my face and leaned back. As I sat there and ate, I surveyed the patrons, trying to recognize someone. Anyone.

For some reason my eyes kept drifting back to the piano player in the corner. The piano was over to my right side just to the left of the saloon door. The man played a fair tune, but even with his back to me and the silly bowler hat he wore, I knew something wasn't right about him. For one thing, he paid more attention to the occupants of the room than to his piano's keyboard like most other players I'd seen tend to do. Not only that, but he also seemed skittish, kind of like a stray cat when someone approaches it.

I took a sip of the beer and began pondering him. The man seemed of average build, and had a small, pencil-thin mustache. He wore a shiny thin brown vest over a faded yellow shirt with two armbands. There was a ring on the middle finger of his left hand. The ring's band had a large blue stone set in it. When he paused to wipe his head, I could tell he was balding and judged him to be in his mid-thirties.

Balding? Then it hit me.

Baldy Jones was wanted in Colorado for robbing a rural couple. Four years ago he'd tied up the young husband, raped the wife, and rode off with the couple's meager savings. If I remembered correctly, there was a $500 bounty out on him. I guess now that he was out of the state, he felt safe.

The question was how to approach him. I could go in hard, up-front-in-his-face and blunt, or I could be clever, friendly, and deceptive. I didn't have much time to waste, so I decided to wing it. I'd just play whatever cards fate dealt me.

I got up slowly, walked over to the piano, and set the beer mug down on its top. "Don't I know you?" I asked curiously.

Jones looked up at me suspiciously but never stopped playing. "I don't think so," he replied, shaking his head.

"Sure I do. I remember now . . . Soapy Johnson and I were talking once and he mentioned you. Jones, ain't it?"

Soapy was a young con man I had heard of. He was developing quite a reputation for himself, unsavory as it might be, but I never actually went after him. I suppose at the time I was too pre-occupied with other cases. Soapy was known all across the territory for bilking old widows out of their life's savings and for running crooked faro games. It was the first outlaw's name that popped into my head and I hoped Jones would recognize it.

The piano player looked up at me and squinted. I could tell the name had rung a bell even though he shook his head. "Don't know him or you."

I leaned in closer. "Look, I'm sure it's you, Jones, and I need a favor. I'm in a big jam."

"Sorry, I cain't help you." He was emphatic.

I took out a double eagle and slapped it on the piano. "Would this help?"

He looked at the coin. "Depends on what you need?" he replied quietly. His hands never once left the keyboard.

"I got a posse and at least one bounty man hot on my trail and I need to get through the pass. You know . . . that one out in Johnson County. I've heard of it, but have never been there. Soapy told me that if someone doesn't know how to get through, they get dead real quick. I thought maybe you could help. I can't risk getting caught. I ain't gonna do no more time!" My tone made me sound desperate.

The piano player shook his head violently and whispered: "Look, I'd like to help, but I can't. If I ever told the wrong person and it got out, all the gold in the hills wouldn't save my skin. I know how those folks operate. Nope, no siree, that's one secret I'm taking to my grave."

At least now I was sure of one thing. Jones knew the way into the pass. I gave it one more try. "Even for a friend of Soapy's? Even for someone on the lam?"

"Son, I wouldn't tell you even if it was for my own mother."

I shook my head and returned the coin to my pocket. "All right, let's do this another way." I slammed the piano cover down. Hard. Right on his fingers.

Baldy screamed, but when I sat down on the edge of the lid his scream caught in his throat and turned to a whimper. "No information, no fingers." I shrugged. "I figure if they're not broken by now, the lack of circulation ought to ruin your music career pretty darn' quick."

Jones's face was twisted in pain. I actually thought he was going to puke. Instead, tears started flowing and he started whining. "Please, God, let go. I'll tell you whatever you want to know."

Once the bartender noticed that the music had stopped, he looked at us, realized what was happening, and started to bend over. Before he could retrieve whatever weapon he had hidden behind the counter, I drew my shotgun and cocked it. I pointed it at him, and then moved it around the room. "This lowlife is my brother-in-law. I come to fetch him home to Sis. It's family business, so back off or eat lead!"

The bartender stood back up, and after a moment's hesitation the rest of the room returned to its normal activity. I stood up and grabbed Baldy Jones by the collar, hauled him up, and ran him out the door. Around the corner was a small alleyway and I pushed him in there, and shoved the shortened express gun under his chin.

"By now I guess you've figured out I ain't one to piss off. You tell me what I need to know, and, if I even see you blink, or if I don't believe you for whatever reason, I'm gonna separate your head from your shoulders with this." I pushed up a little with the shotgun barrel for emphasis.

"It's simple!" he cried. "Once you get to the Hole-in-the-Wall, you tie a bandanna to your horse's bridle. You ride in carrying your rifle or pistol held up high in your left hand. Any lookouts see that, they let you through. If not, you won't stand a chance."

"And getting out?" I asked, pushing his chin up a mite.

"Nobody cares about that. Hell, why would they?"

"That's it? All there is to it is just letting the

look-outs see how you carry your gun and where you tie a lousy bandanna?"

"I swear to God Almighty." Jones whimpered. "But ya gotta do both." Given the situation he was in, I was inclined to believe him.

"Come with me," I said, lowering the shotgun and spinning him around. With the gun at his back and my other hand on his neck, I pushed him out the alley and over to the sheriff's office.

"What are we doing here?" Jones asked, surprised. "I thought you said you were on the run?"

"Sorry," I said, shrugging. "I lied. Only place we're running to is the jail."

Once inside, I found the lawman at his desk, dozing, about as I'd expected. He awoke with a start. I walked Jones right past his desk and shoved the piano player right into a cell. "Get your ass over here, Sheriff, and lock this damn' cell door."

The sheriff got up and hurried over with the key to the lock.

"Who the hell are you? You can't talk to me like that. I'm the law here," he insisted.

I spun around and shoved the sawed-off under his nose. "Really? Then what's this murderer and rapist doing in your town calmly playing the piano like he don't have a care in the world?"

"Him?" the sheriff asked foolishly.

"You see any other piano player around here?"

The sheriff shook his head. "You sure about him?"

"Do your job and check the Wanted posters, if ya don't believe me." I was angry. "Hell, half of them are probably still over there in those unopened envelopes on your damn' desk."

The sheriff looked at the shotgun I still held pointed at him.

"So what do you want out of all this?" he asked quietly

"I'll tell you what you're going to do, Sheriff. You're gonna find the poster on him, and then you are gonna notify the authorities listed on that poster. Then you are gonna keep this man in jail till they come for him. Understand?"

The lawman just nodded silently.

"One more thing. I don't want him out even to take a piss! Feed him soup through the door if you have to, but don't let him out. And don't let anyone . . . and I mean anyone . . . talk to him unless they're wearing a marshal's badge. You understand?"

The lawman stood there dumbly and again just nodded.

"You do that and you can keep the reward all for yourself. That and the bragging rights to this hardened criminal you just caught."

The man looked back at me as I holstered the shotgun. "Reward, huh? Well now, that sounds reasonable."

"And I don't want any discussion as to how he got here," I added. "Any folks from the saloon ask, just tell them you recognized both of us from recent posters. Unfortunately I got away. Understood?"

"That true?" the sheriff asked suspiciously.

"No, you fool. If there was paper out on me, do you think I'd show up here?"

He scratched his chin. "No, I guess not. So what's this all about?"

"I don't want anybody on my back trail, that's all," I said. "I'm heading back south and I don't want to run into any of his friends." It was a lie, but a necessary one.

"Seems like a man like you wouldn't worry much about that."

I leaned right up into his face. "Even Pecos Bill could get dry-gulched or back shot. I'm gonna ask this just once. Am I gonna have to come back here and check on things? Because, know this, Sheriff, I got a real nasty disposition when it comes to being forced to go out of my way."

The lawman gulped and answered quickly: "No, sir. That son-of-a-bitch is gonna stay there till hell freezes over."

As I was walking out the door I added: "And no visitors!"

Chapter Twenty

After a half day out on the trail I stopped to look at the map again. I had drawn two lines. One ran east to west, from the train robbery site to the Hole-in-the-Wall Pass. The other ran north from the fort to a point halfway along the first line. I hoped to reach that point late the next day. I started for my canteen and changed my mind. I picked up the one Corporal Daniels had given me. I took a swig and coughed. It was as strong as I'd tasted in quite a while.

For the most part the weather was pleasant this time of year, but it was beginning to turn chilly a mite early. I took another drink to ward off the cold, or so I justified it, and recapped the canteen. Before riding on, I reconsidered what I was getting myself into.

I realized that once I found the women, I would still have to find a way to get them out alive and all in one piece. I could ride with two or three of them doubled up on my horse and mule but there were supposedly four women. I also knew that we wouldn't get very far riding that way if we were pursued, and, no matter how I figured it, I knew we would be.

If I were to ride through the pass with a string of saddled but riderless horses, I might have too much explaining to do. Besides, I didn't have a string of horses. That's why I had decided back in Bighorn Gulch that it would be necessary to improvise once I found the women. I also knew that would mean either grabbing some fresh horses or stealing a wagon and team. I shook my head in frustration. Nothing I could come up with seemed to work in my favor.

"Go on, Lobo, hunt," I said, sending the dog off to the woods. "At least someone should have some fun once in a while!" I yelled after him. I patted the Appaloosa on the neck. "Come on, son," I said. "We've dawdled enough." I tugged at the lead rope to the jack mule and rode on.

Late in the afternoon of the following day I came up on an old abandoned mining shack. The countryside was loaded with these old cabins, from here all the way to Bannock. I dismounted and arched my back to ease the stiffness. Lobo hadn't returned yet but I wasn't worried. Like I said, he had his own way of doing things.

There was a lean-to out back of the shack where I could unsaddle and stable the horse and mule. It wasn't much, just a few upright poles and some planks thrown over as a roof, but it also had a thin manger nailed to the crossbeams.

I filled the trough with some oats and corn from a sack I carried on the pack mule, and then I slid in a rear plank that would keep the animals inside the makeshift stall. There was an old bucket lying on the ground near the well so I filled it with water and hung it on a peg I found in the lean-to.

I was tired and hungry myself, but if there's one thing a man learns living out on the trail, it's that his horse's needs always come first. I pulled out my new pair of Army binoculars from my saddlebags and had a look around. I saw nothing unusual, so I hung them around my neck, took my rifle and its scabbard from the saddle, put the saddlebags over my shoulder, and walked over to the cabin.

"Anyone to home?" I shouted before kicking in the front door. If you ignored the hoof prints all around the cabin, the amount of dust on the cabin might have led me to believe that it had been vacant for a long time, but when I went inside, it was clearly too tidy to have been unoccupied for very long.

I set my tack down and began to study the surroundings. I went back outside and walked all around the place. I headed to the well and that's when I noticed a small piece of torn fabric stuck to a splinter near the bottom. I couldn't tell if it was from a man's or a woman's clothing, but one thing was sure, it was clean enough to have been torn off recently.

I noticed that the hoof prints had been made by several different horses and saw what appeared to be wagon wheel tracks. There were also droppings all around. The consistency of the manure fit what I believed to be the right time-frame for when the train robbers would have passed this way. Although I don't believe in coincidences, there was an outside chance they could have been made by another group of men. I wanted more evidence to go on.

Once I was back in the cabin, I opened the shutters and aired the place out. I started a fire in the fireplace and dug out a pot and some coffee from my gear. While it was simmering, I found an old broomstick fashioned from some twigs and cleaned up some. I'm not all that neat; it's just that I really hate spider webs.

It was when I was sweeping out the corner where I planned to bed down that I noticed something shiny in the dust pile. I bent down and picked up a small sparkling piece of glass bead. I knew immediately it had fallen or been torn off a woman's dress.

I began slowly walking around the whole cabin, step by step, looking for other clues. Up on a shelf behind an old opened can filled with fat drippings I found a small, hard ribbon tied into a bow. It was the kind often found on top of a woman's shoe. There was no way that was left accidentally. No, it was clearly a message. *We've been here. Help!* It wasn't a written note, but I could read it plain as day, regardless.

So the women had been held here. That meant that I had been right in my assumptions. Given the direction from the water station where the train had been hit to here, a continuing straight line would lead that gang right to that accursed pass in the Big Horn Mountains.

After making the place a little more livable for the night, I washed up with some of the water I had fetched from the well. I used my old skillet to fry up some beans and bacon and washed it down with some of Corporal Daniels's Irish rheumatism remedy.

Lobo hadn't returned yet, so I had little to distract or entertain me in the twilight. I sat, cross-legged, in front of the fireplace, smoking a cigar. As I sat there, watching the flames flicker, it occurred to me that before there was even history this is probably how most folks passed the time at night before they went to sleep. After all, what else was there to do? Watching a fire can be most distracting since no two burn the same. Ever since I can remember, I have enjoyed watching fires, although I learned early on it isn't wise to do so on the trail.

I got jumped once some years back precisely because I was watching the flickering campfire and had lost my night vision. I was preoccupied with my thoughts instead of paying attention to my surroundings. As it turned out, the outlaw I was pursuing had doubled back on me. When I heard twigs snapping, I knew something was up, but when I turned to look around, all I could see for several seconds was the campfire's image still blurring my vision.

I was temporarily blind. Had it not been for Lobo I'd surely have been a goner. That wolf started growling at the same time I heard another branch break, so I shouted—"Lobo, gun!"—and rolled out of the way as he attacked.

Fortunately the gunshot was aimed at where I had been sitting rather than at Lobo. Or rather, I should say it was lucky for Lobo *and* me. The other feller wasn't quite so lucky. He was a stage-coach robber named Jefferson Banks and I had been after him for almost a month. Lobo took him down and perforated him repeatedly until I was finally able to pull him off the man. As bad as it might sound, I will admit to taking my own sweet time about calling off my dog. You see, I've never been too particularly fond of people who try to bushwhack me.

Banks survived, but barely.

That's why now, whenever I'm out on the trail, I tend to sit with my back to the campfire, or at least off to one side of it. I stare at the flames only on occasion. Trust me, it's real easy to get mesmerized by fire. Here in the cabin I didn't think it mattered quite as much. The men I was chasing had already passed through and were long gone. The room's single window didn't offer a good enough view of the fireplace to be a problem for me should anyone peer in. That also meant there was no clear line of fire. Furthermore, the only door to the cabin was bolted shut with a solid sliding plank. For now I was as safe as I would be anywhere.

As I watched the flames jump in the hearth and as the ashes grew long on my cigar, I thought about what was ahead of me. I still had no clue as to how I would get four women away from a gang of fifteen or more cut-throats. Or even get myself back out alive for that matter.

About an hour later I was about to doze off when I heard a short howl followed by a series of scratching noises at the door. I recognized the sounds from the countless times I'd heard them before, so I got up and opened the door to let Lobo in.

The wolf mix bounded into the room and spun around three times before jumping up on me. I chuckled and patted him on the side. "It's good to see you, too, boy, but I'm tired. Get down."

I went over to my bedroll and stretched out. I whistled softly and the big animal walked over and curled down next to me.

"Damn, Lobo, you stink," I said, shaking my head. "You need a bath." He looked up at me and yawned. It was the last thing I remember before drifting off to sleep that night.

Chapter Twenty-One

The next morning, after I'd fed and watered the livestock, I went back to the well, washed up, and filled my canteen. Lobo was acting his usual self, barking and running playfully around in circles. I imagine he must have spotted a squirrel or some other small critter because he suddenly took off toward the woodshed that was out back of the cabin.

I laughed, and then followed him, mostly out of curiosity. There I found him scratching at the bottom of a large crate. He never did find whatever it was he was chasing, but I found something very interesting written on that old wooden box. Big bold lettering indicating the contents: TNT.

I had used enough of the stuff clearing tree stumps back at the ranch to know what I was doing, so I checked the dynamite sticks for signs of sweating. When TNT is bad, it will ooze nitroglycerin. Even a finger full of that liquid nightmare will explode. Maybe the dynamite hadn't been left long or maybe the shed's protection or the crate's packing helped preserve these particular sticks because they still looked good to me.

I didn't know what I would find when I crossed through the Hole-in-the-Wall Pass, but I did know I'd have a lot of company once I was on the other side, and none of it good. There was no doubt in my mind that the contents of that crate would give me a definite advantage. Honestly I don't know why I hadn't thought of it before.

I saddled up the horse and mule and stuffed as much TNT as I could into my pack. I took a final look around, tied off the mule's lead rope, and mounted the big Appaloosa. After whistling to Lobo, I rode out to the northwest.

While it's true that horses leave distinct marks on the ground, I had learned long ago that tracking isn't as simple as just riding behind someone looking for hoof prints. Sure, sometimes you're lucky enough to find an exaggerated horseshoe that leaves a signature, but just as often there are the times you ride over hard rock and can't find a single solitary print.

To be a good tracker you must learn to think like your prey. If the person being pursued is thirsty enough, he might make for the nearest water hole. Maybe you'll have a chance to cut him off there? If the outlaw is in a big hurry to escape, or inexperienced, he might ride straight, fast, and true, but if he is the clever type, he could decide to backtrack, zigzag, or maybe he'll take time to wipe his trail clean.

You learn to judge time and distance by how dry a horse's droppings are or by noticing if there is any rain water in hoof prints that would otherwise be dry. You look to see if the print is dusty with its sides all caved in, or if it's still fresh.

A good tracker asks himself if grass was trampled by the man's boots or by his horse's shoes. Is it still bent, and, if so, in what direction? Has it started straightening up? Same thing for twigs or branches. To the right eyes the distance between hoof prints can indicate size and speed of the horse and rider.

You quickly learn that outlaws on the run almost always watch their backs and occasionally will lay waiting in ambush. Sometimes they'll set up traps such as digging holes in the trail with sharpened sticks inside them to cripple your horse. They then cover the holes up so they look like solid ground. You learn quickly or you die young.

That's why a tracker or bounty man seldom travels in straight lines. If he feels sure about where his prey is ultimately headed, he may veer off the trail and try to cut him off somewhere farther up ahead.

It was about a three days' ride to that pass in Johnson County and fortunately I had lots of sign to follow. When I arrived at the gang's final destination, I stopped under a somewhat scrappy cottonwood tree and surveyed the area with my new binoculars. I could see immediately why this area was considered impregnable.

The narrow pass had a V-shaped notch that ran through an eroded red rock wall mesa that rose high up over the rolling plains and cañons. There were huge red boulders that must have originally fallen from the rock wall and were now scattered around almost everywhere in the valley below.

From a fugitive's point of view it was a perfect set-up. Anyone on the top of that mesa would have a three-hundred-and-sixty degree view and plenty of time to warn others of an approaching posse.

The area was desolate, and far enough away from civilization to provide a safe haven for outlaws on the run. Here and there, scattered among the sage, were Douglas firs and other pine trees, but not enough to provide any kind of deep cover. Mule deer tracks were evident and I had noticed a black bear paw print when I first rode in. Off in the distance a hawk soared. The Cheyennes considered these mountains sacred, but I knew that what I was planning to do would hardly be considered honoring their spirit ancestors.

"No time like the present," I said out loud. There was no one to listen but the wind. I looked at the dog-wolf that was resting in the shade of that tree.

"I'm not taking you with me, Lobo," I said. "There's just too many of them and I'm afraid I might not make it out this time. I don't want anything happening to you." The dog-wolf looked at me with his tail wagging. I'm sure he didn't understand anything I said, so I persisted: "Sorry, boy, but you don't get to go along with me, so go hunt!" I pointed away from the pass. Lobo seemed to hesitate longer than usual and actually whimpered once. Then he trotted off in the direction I'd indicated. Away from the pass. "And stay away!" I yelled once he was out of sight.

I walked over to the Appaloosa, and removed my bandanna. I tied it to the horse's bridle as instructed. "As good a time as any to get shot at, I guess," I said as I mounted up. I checked on the mule's lead rope. "Hope Baldy knew what he was talking about. I don't hanker for no Thirty-Thirty slug in my gut." The horse turned his head to look as me as if to say: "Me, neither."

An hour later we were at the entrance to the Hole-in-the-Wall Pass. I recognized some hoof prints at the entrance as the same as those I had seen back at that miner's shack. I pulled the Springfield from its scabbard and held it up in my right hand. I spurred the horse on and kept looking straight ahead the whole way down the pass.

They say that sometimes as a man is about to die he sees visions. White men talk about their lives flashing in front of them while the Indians hear the voices of their ancestors or envision a shaman. I don't know if that's true or not, but I swear I knew that a rifle was being cocked and leveled at me even though I couldn't see or hear it. I just knew.

The events of the last few days raced through my mind and suddenly I remembered: *Left arm. Baldy Jones said to hold the rifle in the left arm!* I quickly switched my grip on the Springfield, held it up, and shook it a couple of times. That's about when a sentry hidden in the rock face stood up.

"Mister, ya almost made it," he said, chuckling. "To the other side." I didn't know if he was referring to heaven, hell, or the valley beyond, but at that point I didn't care. "You cut it awful close. I even had my finger on the trigger and was starting to squeeze," he said.

"The only side I want to reach is the other side of this pass," I replied nervously. "Can I ride on?"

"Ride on, stranger," he answered, waving his Henry rifle. "Oh, and 'less you want to get shot offen that horse, remember to keep your rifle pointed straight up."

I rode on ahead, scanning the rock face for anything that might indicate another sentry. Twice I thought I saw the sun reflecting down off something metallic, but my long-distance eyesight wasn't good enough for me to be positive and I didn't want to use binoculars with armed men watching me from the rocks above.

When I finally made it out of the pass, I was met by another guard. "Hold up there!" he ordered, pointing a Winchester at me.

"What's your problem?" I asked angrily.

He levered a shell. "Just checkin'," he replied calmly. "Where you headed? Which group?" he asked firmly. I stared at him with a blank look on my face.

I noticed that the pass behind him opened into small valleys with several paths leading into them. Apparently there were multiple outlaw gangs using this place for their hide-outs. I had no idea how to answer the man, but I remembered a name one of the passengers on the train had overheard the robbers use. I knew that at this range even with the Springfield already in my left hand I couldn't drop it level and fire in time to avoid his pointblank shot. Besides, if I shot my way in, I'd never get out.

"Hank's group," I answered. I swear my heart stopped beating for a full minute.

The guard relaxed a mite and lowered the Winchester. "All right, take the left fork and keep on for a half mile. Take you straight into camp."

"Keep your powder dry," I said, nodding to him as I rode by. Once out of hearing range I added: "You son-of-a-bitch."

By now I was sure I was in the right place, but who this Hank fellow might be was anybody's guess. I didn't remember any posters out on anyone with that first name. At least not locally. But whoever he was, it now seemed apparent that Hank must be one of the leaders of the gang that had kidnapped those women.

The cañon beyond the pass opened up into a green pasture that made for good grazing. Scattered along the way were small cattle herds that I knew had to have been rustled.

About a half an hour later I came to a sign that was carved into the shape of an arrow. Across the front in painted dirty white letters it read BROKEN WILLOW CAMP. At the end of the path was a huddle of a place. It was a hodge-podge mixture of log cabins, ramshackle false store fronts, and a collection of Sibley tents.

Sibleys were old Army tents that sort of resembled Indian teepees because of a cowl that was built over a central pole. This allowed smoke and heat to escape out the top. The tents stood about twelve feet high and about eighteen feet in diameter and in a pinch they could house about a dozen men. As I rode by, I saw that some of them had been sewn together to make more room for tables, cots, and the like. My horse's hoofs kicked up small dust swirls as I made my way slowly along the main street.

There weren't many bystanders around but the few men that were lingering outside all eyed me suspiciously. I couldn't help but notice that, as I passed by, one of them hurried back inside one of the larger wooden structures. It had letters on the side of the building written in crooked white wash that read SALOON.

I continued on to what passed for the camp's livery. It was a large barn built of unevenly cut wooden planks with a small branch-and-cut-log corral off to the right. Out front there was a short fat man with a gray beard who was shoveling hay into a broken-down, three-wheeled wagon.

"Can I leave my horse and mule here?" I asked.

"Naw," the man replied. "I built this barn exclusively for the personal use of the Grand Duke of Russia and his royal family."

I actually smiled at his sarcasm. "Well, I ain't royalty, but I do pay with cash."

"Might make an exception. You staying long?" he asked. I looked at him without answering. In these parts it was rather uncommon to be questioned by a stranger.

"Don't intend to winter here if that's what you're getting at," I finally replied. "If you gotta know, I intend to stay just long enough to let the dust settle. You got a problem with that?"

The man took a small step back and raised his palms up. "No. No problem at all, mister. Just trying to figure the livestock's rations."

"Right. Sure you are," I replied with obvious disbelief. "Just see to it my horse and mule get their fair share." As an afterthought I added: "And remember, I'll be back to check on them. Anyone goes near my horse or the mule and his pack, I'll cut off his fingers, one by one. Understood?"

The liveryman nodded rapidly. "Sure. Like I said, no problem."

I debated for a moment and decided to leave the rifle in its scabbard. In spite of past experiences, I doubted I'd be doing much long-distance shooting here in town. Lugging it around would create too many problems. I reached in my pocket and tossed the man a coin. My stomach growled. "Where can I get something to eat around here?" I asked.

The liveryman pointed to a long tent about halfway up the street on the left. I unbuttoned my jacket, took a look around, and then headed over to the place he'd indicated. When I got to the food tent, I noticed a small blackboard nailed to a pole. In chalk letters it read:

> Today's Special. Same as yesterday and the day before that. Stew—75¢. Take it or leave.

"Better be damn' good stew at that price," I muttered to myself, even though I sincerely doubted it would be.

I sat down at the end of a long wooden table. Ten or so men were already lined up on both sides of the table, eating their lunch. Actually shoveling their lunch would be a more accurate description of what they were doing at the time.

An attractive but rather heavy-set, middle-aged woman came over and handed me a bowl. I took a clean handkerchief from my pocket and wiped it down. The woman looked at me suspiciously. "Fussy, are we?" She appeared to be about forty-five years old or so and wore an apron over a discolored and tattered calico dress. Although I couldn't be positive, I felt sure she didn't fit any of the descriptions I'd been given of the women taken from the train.

"No offense, miss," I replied, "just like to flavor my own food."

The woman went back to the rear of the tent and ladled out some nondescript stew into the bowl. I thought I recognized a carrot and maybe a wild onion, but I was probably being overly optimistic. I leaned over and sniffed the bowl. My nose wrinkled and I swear it made my eyes water. Suddenly I wasn't as sure as I was before I sat down that I was really all that hungry.

"Ketchup's over at the end of the table," she said, pointing with the ladle.

I tried to summon a smile. "Thanks, miss. That'll be fine."

One of the other men snickered as she left. "'Miss,' he says. Catch that?"

The man off to his right laughed and leaned over toward me. "Hell, Swagger Hips ain't been a 'miss' since Christ was crucified."

I nodded my head. "Still, it's never a good idea to upset the person who's serving your meal. Food may be bad enough as it is, but you never know what else might be added if you're rude to the help."

The two men stopped chuckling and glanced down at their bowls suspiciously. I smiled to myself but I'd recognized her nickname. I'd read about her several times in the past. Instead of being some middle-aged woman kidnapped and forced into servitude in this outlaw town, Swagger Hips Sally was actually one of them. She had a list of crimes going back twenty years, including prostitution, stabbing at least two men, and for running con-artist rings in at least three states. Sally must have had quite a fall to end up dishing out stew in a place like Broken Willow.

When she was younger, the word was she was a real looker. One of Swagger Hips Sally's most famous routines was to set up a shop in some big city like Denver, and then wait for married men to come in. She would flirt with each of the men until one of them took her up on the offer. She would then retire with the mark being conned to a previously arranged hotel room. Then, when they were in that perfect and most compromising of positions, her jealous husband would suddenly barge in and demand satisfaction.

To the not-so-innocent victim's relief satisfaction meant money to pay off the supposedly offended husband. In other words, pay and the big angry jealous man will go away. The threat in effect was that, if you didn't pay her husband what he demanded, he would not only beat you up, but would also spill the beans to your wife about the whole affair.

Almost always the mark chose to pay up and it was rumored that Sally had amassed a small fortune over a very long time. Of course, all good things come to an end, and from what they tell me she eventually tried to con a private detective who had rather good boxing skills. I don't know for sure exactly what finally became of the man who pretended to be her husband, but from what they tell me, it wasn't very pretty.

As it turned out, the stew really did need ketchup to help get it down. After lunch I lit a cigar and nonchalantly surveyed my surroundings. It wasn't really that large a camp or even all that crowded, but considering my position the numbers didn't have to be very big. I was here all by my lonesome with nobody to turn to for help. Not in this place.

I pulled my jacket collar up and starting walking down what passed for a street. The first few cabins were spaced about ten to twenty yards apart and were mostly of single-story log construction. I didn't notice any activity around the cabins so I continued on toward the large two-story building I had noticed when I rode in.

There was a long rectangular sign over the front doorway with hand carved letters that read: THE WATERING HOLE. I smiled when I read the sign. It stood to reason that in a place like this the biggest building in town would be the saloon. Around the sides and out back of the bar were several large tents with their flaps down. I could only imagine what sordid activities they were intended for.

In the Beadle pocket novels that have become so popular the local saloon always has those big bat-wing doors that swing open and music is always playing loudly from within. Whoever built this place must not have known how to read because this entrance had a large, single, solid wood door and I heard no music coming from inside. I took a slow, deep breath, opened the door, and went in.

Almost as soon as I entered the place, I had a pistol shoved in the back of my head and was escorted over to a table in the corner. Two men were seated there. One was tall with brown hair and a thin mustache. He appeared to be between fifty and sixty years of age and had a small scar on his left cheek. He wore a long cotton coat, a black flat-brimmed hat, and a brace of Remington pistols, butts forward in cross-draw, Slim Jim holsters.

The other man was more widely built, had black hair, and seemed to me to be in his mid-fifties. He was clean-shaven and wore his hat ten-gallon style with a large red bandanna tied around his neck. I couldn't help but notice he looked at me with a slight sideways bend to his head, looking up more with his right eye, as if he had a pain in his side. It seemed as if his head was glued to his left shoulder. At his waist he had on a wide cartridge belt, and in one of those smaller, cut-down holsters he carried one of the newer Colt Single Action Army pistols called Peacemakers.

This particular pistol was probably a .45-caliber five-inch model, but it had been fancied up with nickel plating and stag-horn grips. I remember at the time wondering whom he had stolen it from.

"Can I help you gentlemen?" I asked. I tried to sound as calm and collected as was possible under the circumstances. I knew there was an outside chance that I might have been recognized, but doubted it. While it's true that a man in my line of work can develop a reputation, I always worked alone and most of the men I went after were either dead or had been put away for a very long time.

I realized that even outlaws have friends and it was possible that some of my prisoners had described me to others. I really didn't think that was the case here. I hadn't said, done, or given away anything specifically to single me out. No, this was more likely going to be a we're-the-bosses-here talk or maybe a just-who-the-hell-are-you inquisition. As it turned out it was a little of both.

"My name is Henry Clayton Thompson," the taller, thinner man with the Remingtons said first. "My associate here"—he gestured toward the other man—"is Royce Dunbar. We run Broken Willow and we are both a mite, shall we say, *particular* about who we want settling here."

"Or who we allow to visit," the other, more muscular man said. "So just who are you and what gives you the right to ride the pass?"

I was prepared for this and after the appropriate amount of respectful hesitation, I fumbled around in my pants pocket for a folded and weathered piece of paper. I handed it to the one who had identified himself as Henry Thompson. I assumed this was the man called Hank I had heard about.

He unfolded the paper, read it, and showed it to the other man. "Robbery and murder," he said loud enough so those around the table could hear. "Wells, Fargo. Very impressive."

I stood there, expressionless.

Hank handed me back the paper. "Broken Willow has high standards and a reputation to uphold." I was a little puzzled until he added: "I think you'll fit in fine." He motioned to the man who held the gun to my back. "That'll do . . . he's all right." I breathed a small sigh of relief.

Turning to the bartender, Royce added: "Pour this man a beer. First one's always on the house." The cynic in me assumed that this was because the rest of the drinks would be twice what you'd pay anywhere else.

"Thanks," I offered. "Had a tough time getting here, but if what they say is true about this place, I just might stay a while. By the way, just where does one stay while here in town?"

"End of the street opposite the big cabin marked Armory and Hardware is a row of tents," Hank explained. "You can rent one from Curly Avery. He usually hangs around the store playing checkers with the manager. Can't miss him . . ."

"Because of his hair?" I interrupted.

Royce laughed. "You'd think so, but no. His lack of it."

I nodded back at him. "Got it." Looking around the saloon, I noticed three women serving tables. There were supposed to be four but these three fit the descriptions of the women from the train. Even so, I'd still have to make sure.

"Didn't expect to find such attractive women here," I commented.

Hank looked over at them and smiled. "You know, when a man gets older he begins to think about leaving something behind to remember him by."

"That so?" I said, puzzled by the remark.

"Yep. Ya see, someday this here's going to be a big town and I want to be remembered by it. And for that we'll need women to help build it. Having some ladies in a town makes men want to stay, and things seem more civilized when there's womenfolk around." I nodded, trying to appear as understanding as possible.

"What you see around here, well . . . this is just the beginning. We intend to grow this place up right. Royce is the town sheriff and I, of course, am the duly appointed mayor of Broken Willow."

Duly appointed? The way Hank talked I was surprised he hadn't named the place Hanksville.

I looked up at the second floor of the saloon. "So, the rooms up there, are they available for . . . female entertainment?"

Hank Thompson looked uncomfortable for some reason and glanced over at his partner, Royce. To my eye he appeared angry. "Perhaps later, but not for now," he said. "That was to be the plan, but we have put such things on . . . shall we say . . . temporary hold. We had a minor incident recently that unfortunately decreased our town's population. Maybe later."

I didn't like the sound of that. Something was clearly amiss. "Well, then, you won't mind if I just have a friendly conversation with one or the other, do you? You know, if the opportunity arises," I asked harmlessly.

Royce looked nervously at Hank and answered first. "Just keep it on the first floor and it shouldn't be no problem. Lot of competition, though," he observed.

"Oh, I don't aim to compete," I assured him. "It's just that I haven't seen a pretty face in a month of Sundays and thought it might be nice to socialize a bit."

"Socialize all you like," Hank said. "But just one other thing. As long as you are in Broken Willow, there will be no cheating or stealing or the like. We aim to run a tight ship, and trust me, Royce can be a real effective first mate, if you know what I mean."

Royce Dunbar patted his Colt Peacemaker loud enough to be heard.

"Honor among thieves, that sort of thing?" I asked.

Hank nodded. "Something like that."

"Thanks," I said, tipping up the brim of my hat. "I think I'll go get that free beer you mentioned."

"Take her slow," Royce replied.

As I walked over to the bar, I couldn't help but notice that his hand was still tapping the butt of his pistol.

While at the bar I took a closer look around. The walls of the saloon were chinked with old newspaper and mud packed in between the logs, but in general the building seemed solid enough. There were several thin ropes stretched across the ceiling from which hung various lanterns. I counted eight large windows to let light in and all were built with shutters. That was a very good idea. Anyone who'd spent a single winter in this area knew the importance of closing a room off to wind, rain, and snow.

There were about twenty or so tables in the place, but not all had chairs. Somebody had simply cut down a few rain barrels and added planking on top to sit on. Seated at the tables and standing next to me at the bar were approximately thirty or so men of varying ages. Even at a quick glance I recognized at least three men with Wanted posters out on them. I knew from the get-go that the odds would be stacked against me, but the numbers here in town went far beyond what I had expected. I'd have to get very clever real quick.

I watched the women for a while. They were wandering around the saloon, bringing the men beer and occasionally being forced to sit with them. They all had a look of profound sadness that touched even a hard-ass like myself. I quickly realized how difficult it would be to get them alone as there were at least ten men for every girl.

I took a gulp of my beer and stared at it, surprised at how good it tasted. "Not bad," I said to the bartender.

"It's the mountain water the beer's brewed in," he replied.

"Really? Brewing it in mountain water makes it taste better?"

"Why not?" the bartender asked, resting his arms on the counter. "Wouldn't be surprised if someday brewing with mountain spring water becomes famous all over the country."

"Right," I replied. "And when that day comes, they'll be selling beer in cans like peaches."

The bartender laughed loudly. "That's a good one! Canned beer. Hah!"

I dropped a couple of coins on the bar top. "Until then, how about another mug?"

"Coming right up. Canned beer." He chuckled again. "Got to remember that one."

Off to my left four men were playing poker and in the far corner an older cowboy in a cowhide vest was strumming a juice harp and tapping his foot to the tune. I had no idea what song he was playing but he seemed happy. Happy? That set me to thinking. I decided that I too needed to get happy, so I downed a few more beers in quick succession, left the counter, and started stumbling around the saloon.

I didn't harm anyone and didn't knock over anything serious, but I wasn't exactly steady on my feet, either. Sooner or later I bumped into one of the girls. I knew for sure who she was. Eileen looked just like she did in the picture the sergeant had signed for me.

"Hey, watch out. You stepped on my foot," she squealed.

I removed my hat in an exaggerated motion. "My sincerest apologies, my lady." I replaced my hat after first removing the picture from the inside crown with my hidden hand. It was now secretly nestled in my palm.

"Please get away from me. You're drunk."

Out of the corner of my eye I noticed Royce sliding his chair out as if he were about to rise. With my back to him, I grabbed her hand and kissed it. "Again I deeply regret any inconvenience to you." I quietly added— "Eileen."—and from underneath flipped the picture up into her hand. "May nothing but good fortune come to you from now on," I added loudly.

I have to hand it to her, she didn't even look down at her hand. I backed away and smiled. "Hope to see you again under better circumstances." I winked and returned to the bar. Thankfully Royce relaxed when I went back to nursing my drink.

I wasn't worried about letting the cat out of the bag. If anyone were to find the picture that I had passed her, they would assume it was nothing important. Even if she had previously been searched, they would probably just think it was something they had missed. Eileen, however, would understand, especially since her brother's name was on the back. It wasn't written down but she would surely get the message: *Help is on the way.* Now the only problem I faced was figuring out how the hell that help would arrive. Well, maybe not the only problem.

Chapter Twenty-Two

After an appropriate amount of time had been wasted at the bar, I finally stumbled over to the door. Turning to the table where Hank and Royce were seated, I slurred my speech slightly. "Tents behind the Avery? Hardware right?"

Hank smiled and shook his head. "Curly Avery. Behind the Armory and Hardware store."

"Right, Avery . . . Armory," I said, staggering out of the saloon.

Once outside, I straightened up and took a couple of deep breaths. I don't know if it was more to clear my head of the beer or to get the stench of that place out of my lungs.

I walked slowly toward the hardware store. It was across the street, and on my way there I continued planning a way out of this mess. My first impulse had been to grab a couple of horses and somehow race out of town. Now I realized that would never work out. With such a large group of outlaws chasing us, it was a sure bet I wouldn't get very far with those women in tow. We would also need supplies for the trail and that meant overloading the pack mule, which would also slow us down.

Putting two and two together, the problem was simple. The answer wouldn't be. First I had to find a way to get the women alone, and then steal them away sight unseen. Then we had to ride away with enough supplies for the group. I figured at least a five-day ride and I didn't know how well or even if these women could ride. It soon became apparent that I'd need a wagon, but that meant traveling slower and leaving a bigger and more obvious trail for the men who would be following us at a gallop.

I was still dealing with those concerns when I entered the hardware store. It was fairly spacious for a log cabin and had quite an impressive assortment of supplies on its shelves. The rifle rack sported a wide variety of weapons. In the corner near the potbellied stove two men were seated at a small table, playing checkers.

"One of you Avery?" I asked.

A bald-headed man looked up and took a corncob pipe from his mouth. "Yeah, I am. Whatcha want?"

I exaggerated the facts a bit. "Hank sent me over here. Said for you to fix me up with a tent."

Curly looked me over. "That so? You know Hank Thompson?"

"We go back some," I lied. "You got any accommodations available?"

"You got any money?" he asked

"Enough for a lousy tent and cot. You gonna play games all day or do I get a room?"

"Hold your horses." Curly started to rise. "You'll get one if Thompson says so, but my stuff ain't lousy."

"Better not be," I grumbled. "Say, this place is pretty well stocked for being so far out of the way," I said as I looked the store over again.

"We make out all right," Curly's friend said.

"Damn, will ya look at all this. Canned fruit, a stove, bridle headstalls, reins and bits, gunpowder barrels, clothing. Quite an assorted stock," I said casually. It went without saying most of it was probably stolen. "How the hell did you manage to get all this through the pass, so far out in territory? Even my mule couldn't haul it."

"We have a Conestoga, a light buckboard, and an old stagecoach out back that we use to bring in supplies from time to time," Curly explained.

The women had been brought all that way here into town by wagon. Made sense to consider using one for the same thing only in the opposite direction.

"Interesting. So if I were to decide to stay here but needed to go back for the rest of my necessities, would you rent me one?"

"One of the wagons? Nope. See the way it usually works, anything you don't carry in, you buy here."

That rule meant I'd have to plan on taking one by stealth or force. Neither option appealed to me.

"Right," I said. "Had to ask anyway. Now about that tent?"

After paying Curly for three days up front, he went outside and pointed out the tent I was assigned to.

"Thanks. I'll go get my bedroll at the livery and be back."

"Suit yourself, I ain't your pa," Curly replied, putting the pipe back in his mouth. I turned my back on him and returned to the livery.

"Just getting my bedroll," I told the liveryman. His name was Craig Phelps and I later learned he was wanted for back-stabbing a friend in

Abilene after losing to him in a poker game. Phelps had lived here for the past three years, running his livery with stolen horses.

"Where'd you put my tack?" I asked.

Phelps indicated a small room in back of his shed, and while I was pretending to straighten up my duffel, I located a couple of harnesses that could be used on a wagon, if and when the time came. Even with my big mule I would need at least two horses to pull a wagon over hard terrain with four other passengers. I shook my head. Mulling it over, I also realized that once it was discovered that the women were gone whoever came after us would be riding hard and fast. One wagon carrying that many wouldn't get very far. I knew I'd have to think of something else to stop those pursuers dead in their tracks. I was worn out and decided to sleep on it.

I threw my bedroll and saddlebags over my shoulders and went back to my tent. As much as I wanted to get this mission over with quickly, I knew that it wouldn't be smart to start sneaking around so soon after arriving in town. Getting caught snooping around at night would create far too much suspicion.

As I threw myself down on the cot, I realized that tomorrow didn't promise to be an easier day. All things considered, when you walk through the valley of the shadow of death, you are within a shadow's length of death.

Chapter Twenty-Three

In the Army Colonel Grierson had taught me the basic steps to carrying out a military operation successfully. First the commander in charge had to have intelligence, and not just the brainy smart kind. By *intelligence* the colonel meant finding out as much information as you can about the enemy. You have to consider things like the number of enemy troops, how they are positioned, how many supplies they have, and their plan of attack. All these are described as intelligence information.

This sort of informative detail was often obtained by scouting, by interrogating captive prisoners, or by utilizing spies. I had scouted out part of the town but there was still much to see and learn. I had no spies with me, but if I could somehow manage to get the women alone, I was sure they would provide me with additional information about the goings on here in Broken Willow.

The next step was to ready your men for the mission. This meant arming them, and making sure they were well supplied with food, water, clothing, and ammunition. I knew now that I would need a wagon to carry out our escape. I figured I'd simply pack in whatever supplies I could round up and then pile everyone and everything in the back. What I would need besides the wagon were extra horses or mules to pull it. How to get them was still an unknown factor. Then I would have to deal with the pursuers.

If I learned anything from Grierson's raid, it was to do the unexpected. So far I was not under suspicion and was relatively free to come and go. It was obvious that the women were a prize possession, but I didn't believe they would be heavily guarded since they had nowhere to go for help. Unfortunately at this point I could see nothing clever about simply racing through the pass and making for safety in a wagon. Nope, I would need an ace in the hole to pull off something unexpected.

I left my tent, but the thought of returning to Sally's for breakfast turned my stomach, so I walked into the hardware store. Curly was nowhere to be found but the other fellow was. He was middle-aged and wore a pair of small spectacles.

"Any coffee to be had?" I asked.

"Over on the stove," he replied. "Help yourself."

"Thanks . . . er . . . ?" I hesitated.

"Just call me Flip," he replied, wiping down the counter with a dirty rag.

I poured myself some hot coffee into one of the tin cups that were hanging on a peg next to the stove. "Not bad. Much obliged . . . Flip." I walked around the store, picking up and inspecting assorted items, and slowly nursed the coffee.

Near the back door I noticed an old pack saddle. "Hey, this might come in handy for my mule," I said, lying through my teeth. "Let me get in here and get a better look." I had to move the gun-powder barrels out of the way in order to take a closer look. They were what I was really interested in, so I shoved them over near the doorway. I turned the saddle over and shook my head.

"Interested?" the shopkeeper asked.

"Close but no ceegar," I replied. "Too much rot in the rawhide. Let's see what else you got. Don't mind, do ya?"

"That's what it's here for," he answered.

"Might be able to use this lariat," I commented, picking up a length of rope.

"Sorry but that's not a lariat," Flip explained. "It's blasting line. Primer cord. Miners use it to time their charges."

"Oh, thanks, anyway." I tossed the curled rope over on top of the powder barrels. I picked up a large pocket knife I didn't need and put five canteens on the counter.

"You planning on riding through Death Valley?" Flip asked.

I laughed overly hard and shook my head. "Nah, nothing like that. It's just that on one job the damn' posse put a round through my water bag.

Since then I don't take any chances. Besides, I always carry an extra one for refreshment other than water, if you know what I mean."

Flip smiled. "For that you'd have to go over to the saloon. Hank don't cotton much to competition and I gotta pay a percentage to him and Royce as it is."

"Sweet set-up they got here," I commented, while pouring myself another cup of coffee. It really was pretty good. Besides, gathering intelligence and killing time were often the same thing. As it was I needed to wait till later to get close to the women.

"Known Hank and Royce long?" I asked.

The shopkeeper shook his head. "I showed up about two years ago and they were already here. Fact is, I don't really know how long they've been around."

"So they get a cut of everything that goes on around here?"

Flip nodded. "That Hank, he's a sharp one. I'm no stranger to the Owl Hoot Trail and I've seen many come and go in my time, but Thompson's as slick as they come. Got a mean streak as well, but he don't show it often. The other one . . ."

"Royce?"

"Yeah." He nodded. "Royce Dunbar. Now he's a piece of work, too. As fast on the draw as I've ever seen and someone to watch out for. He can be downright ruthless if the need be."

"And Henry Thompson determines when the need be?"

"Right. Some of those setting up business in Broken Willow thought they was pretty tough, too, but any that objected to Hank's percentage didn't live long. Hell's bells, when they went up against Thompson and Dunbar, they didn't live long enough to say . . . Davy Crockett at the Alamo. And it warn't purty, either."

"I'll have to remember that." An idea came to me, so I decided to lay the groundwork. "I was thinking I might settle down here where no lawman can reach me. Maybe bring in a couple of gaming tables, roulette wheels, and the like. I know where some is stashed. I'd need a wagon, though."

"I don't know. You might make a go of it. Don't know about the wagon. Have to think it over. Talk to Curly maybe."

"Well, you do that. Think it over and let me know. Till then I'll just check out the competition. Keep it to yourself, would ya?"

"Sure thing. Don't hurt to consider possibilities."

"Never does. Thanks again for the coffee," I added as I went outside.

I began to explore the town. It was built in a horseshoe shape with the open end facing the pass. At the closed end of the horseshoe was the livery. Many of the buildings were unmarked but here and there I noticed signs indicating a blacksmith, a barber who doubled as a dentist, and the leather smith shop.

The saloon was open but I doubted the women would be there this early and I didn't want to be too obvious. I was still trying my best to plan my way out of town in such a way as not to get captured, maimed, or killed. So far the odds were all against my getting even close to pulling that off.

By now I knew our escape route would have to be a retreat back through the pass. I studied the valley beyond Broken Willow and realized there was no way out and no safe haven anywhere in that direction.

For a while I had considered stampeding the outlaws' horses in order to gain enough time to make our escape and cover our tracks, but it soon became obvious to me that wouldn't work at all. The majority of the horses were scattered all around the camp. Some were tied to hitching rails, some were in the corral next to the livery, while others grazed in the pasture out in the valley behind the town. They were never all together.

No matter how we sneaked through the pass there would always be enough horses to chase us down and I still couldn't be sure all the girls knew how to ride well enough to outrun those who might pursue us.

I knew I could trail the mule fast enough, but

loading him down with enough supplies for all of us to get back to safety was going to be a close call. The more I thought about it the more sense using a wagon made. Unfortunately I also realized it would slow us down so much I would have to make some sort of allowance to prevent us from being overtaken.

I considered the guards at the pass, but it stood to reason they would only worry about men who were entering. They were put there to prevent lawmen from penetrating the pass, so why would they worry about anyone who was leaving? Unless, of course, they spotted the women. Then they would know for sure something was wrong. It was a sure bet that they knew the plan was to keep those girls in town for good. That would be a problem if the women were spotted. The more I thought about it the more complicated it all became.

Eventually I wandered over to the Watering Hole Saloon and went in. It was still too early in the day for a drink, even for me. The girls were nowhere in sight so I looked around for a way to blend in and pass the time. At one of the tables off to the right a poker game was in play, so I went over to see if I could get in on it.

"Private game or can any loser join?" I asked.

One of the players was an old man with a long gray beard, wearing a patch over his left eye. Even without memorizing all the Wanted posters going back to the beginning of time, I knew immediately the man was Barney Blake. Lawmen had been talking about him and his eye patch for years. It had a single diamond right in the middle for decoration. Blake was wanted in several states for cattle rustling, murder, and other assorted crimes. Some of the crimes went back years. It seemed to me that aside from the kidnapped women there wasn't a single person in this god-forsaken place who was worth a plugged nickel.

"Always can use some fresh blood in the game," another of the players replied. "Pull up a chair and make yourself comfortable."

After quickly catching up on the table rules, I put some coin down in front of me and anted up. The more I thought about it, the more I liked the idea of claiming I'd need to buy or borrow a wagon in order to bring in gambling tables. It would appeal to the nature of the town's inhabitants and made enough sense to be believable. I would, however, need to present myself as someone with decent gambling abilities. Fortunately once again I had Sergeant Hackworth to thank for schooling me.

Sarge didn't get to be top dog in the Army without learning how to play cards, and after he retired to our ranch, we passed many a night playing poker. He soon taught me how to recognize a bottom deal, how to mark cards, and how to spot things like mirrored rings and sleeve devices for throwing cards.

The group at my table were playing fairly evenly, which is to say they were all trying to cheat each other in some form or another. I folded some hands early on, took only modest pots on others, and passed the time waiting for just the right hand.

After three hours of play the girls entered the room through the back door. They all had the same expressions of extreme sadness on their faces. I noticed they still wore the same dresses as before but it seemed to me they were trying to maintain an air of cleanliness.

Hank Thompson walked in right behind them. I studied his face in exact detail and subconsciously tapped the shotgun at my side. I watched him point out a small stage that had been set up in the back of the saloon. Three girls climbed its two steps and lined up in a group. I wondered what had become of the fourth woman.

Five men appeared from the other side of the room and went over to the side of the stage where a small piano had been positioned. One of the men sat down and the others reached behind the piano and pulled out a banjo, a violin, a guitar, and a bass fiddle. They started playing, and then the girls, after a forceful cough from Thompson, began to sing.

They were nowhere near as good as the normal singers were in such places, but I reminded myself they were not professional saloon girls and were scared to death. I was both saddened and furious but at the moment there was very little I could do. I noticed one of the trio nudging the other, and the girls began looking my way. I caught them focusing on me and I shook my head as subtly as I could to stop their staring.

I quickly looked back down and resumed play. Eventually I had just the right combination of cards. One of the men folded his hand early, the other, a big, bearded man named Jamison, threw down three queens, and Blake smiled and showed his hand. Three eights and two kings, a full house. As he was reaching for the pot, I touched his hand and dropped four sevens.

The pot was large enough to make me look good and prove my gambling savvy, but not large enough to provoke a gunfight. Besides, Blake had been cheating, too. As far as he could tell, I had simply gotten lucky. Since I had made no earlier protests about all the good hands he drew, I hoped he wouldn't suspect I was on to his bottom dealing and playing to it. He looked at me long enough to make me tense up, but finally smiled and allowed me to take the pot.

"Nicely played," he remarked.

"Well, everyone gets lucky now and then." I relaxed.

"Iffen you believe in luck," he stated coldly.

I played the next two hands, purposely losing a modest amount each time, and then got up from the table.

"I'm not walking away rich but at least I killed some time without having to pay for it," I commented.

"Still lots more time left in the day," Jamison responded.

"True, but I need to stretch my legs, and, besides, I want to talk to Thompson."

"Be careful of that one," Blake said quietly. "No back up or give in him. He runs this place tighter than Dick's hatband. Even Royce treads lightly around Hank, and he's meaner than a pit viper."

I touched the brim of my hat and nodded. "Right. Got it."

I walked over to the bar just as the girls were finishing up the small repertoire of songs I was willing to bet they'd been forced to learn. I proceeded to order a beer, and then walked to the far end near the stage. As the three came down off the stage and passed by, I raised my beer mug and said in praise: "Nicely done. Reminds me of good times with my Uncle Ben back home in Grierson's tavern."

The tallest of the three, obviously Colonel Grierson's niece, quickly put her hand to her mouth to stifle a gasp. I turned away. With all eyes in the room on them, I couldn't just let them stop to carry on a private conversation. Any message would have to be passed to them by me very carefully.

I walked over to Thompson at the other end of the bar and offered to buy him a drink.

"In this place anyone who's buying's got something on their mind," he said firmly. "Let's have it."

"All right," I replied. "I've been pondering the layout here and I think I might be able to help. You scratch my back, I scratch yours."

"My back's just fine as it is. What did you have in mind?" he asked.

I took a swig of the beer and wiped my face on my sleeve. "I'm thinking I'm not getting any younger, and sooner or later the law, even as bungling as it usually is, might actually catch up with me. No way in hell I'm doing any more time in the hoosegow."

"Chance you take in our line of work," Thompson replied, shrugging. He called the bartender over and ordered a beer. "Put it on my friend's tab," he ordered. "So you were saying something about scratching my back?"

I nodded. "I have access to some gaming tables that I think might fit nicely into this set-up. After all, what's a town without a full-fledged professional gambling operation? I've got a wheel of fortune, craps tables, roulette, the whole works. You help me get started, and I'm willing to give you a piece of the action . . . as mayor."

Hank Thompson looked at me, long and hard. "Oh, I'd get a piece of the action whether you were willingly offering or not," he remarked with a smirk. He thought a moment before nodding in agreement. "Might be a good idea at that. Men can get mighty bored just playing cards all winter. So what do you need from me besides my permission?"

"Well, the problem is I need a wagon to go get them, and there are only a few in town. Apparently Curly and his friend Flip have a lock on 'em."

"Why don't you just get one in the town where the tables are stored in?"

I shook my head. "Who says they're being kept in a town?"

He took off his hat and scratched his head. "So where are they?"

"Hidden out of sight," I said. "Well hidden. Won't tell no one where for obvious reasons, but I will tell you that two years back a wagon train of . . . shall we say ill repute . . . got robbed and all its goods removed to a safe place. Included in that lot were all the trappings to set up a full-scale gambling hall. I know where that lot was stashed. Problem is I need a wagon to haul it and I don't want to buy one in some town where my picture's plastered on every barbershop and sheriff's office. Get the idea?"

Hank smiled, and then laughed. "Don't flatter yourself. I doubt you're that notorious. But I do see your predicament." He nodded again. "All right. I'll talk to the men and get them to lend you their Conestoga and a couple of draft horses. Just lend, mind you. You don't bring it back and there will be hell to pay, I promise you." He then extended his hand. "The town cut is twenty-five percent."

"Ten percent," I replied, extending mine. I didn't give a hoot in hell what it would be, but I needed to sound convincing.

"Twenty," he said after a moment's hesitation.

"My tables. Fifteen and it's a deal." We shook on fifteen percent and agreed I'd get the wagon by the next day.

Chapter Twenty-Four

I walked out of the saloon and right into the middle of a fire fight. Directly in front of the building and out in the center of the street Royce Dunbar was squared off in front of another man, one I'd never seen before. Even at a quick glance it was obvious what was about to happen. I stopped and backed up a step, my right hand resting on the stock of my shotgun.

"Nobody, but nobody steals in Broken Willow!" Dunbar ranted. He was furious.

The other man, tall and thin with a heavy overcoat and a black, flat-brim hat was holding a Henry lever-action rifle. "You're crazy. I didn't

195

take nothing what weren't mine," he said. "It was just my share is all." He looked around the street nervously.

"You knew the deal all along," Dunbar said angrily. "Anything we took from that train stays locked up until Hank Thompson personally divvies it up. Not until. You knew that when you signed up for the job."

Apparently the thin man had broken into some storeroom where the spoils of their last robbery were stashed and tried to take his cut and leave. Royce must have caught him at it. I wouldn't want to face a man cradling a rifle with just a holstered handgun, but Dunbar never flinched. The man with the rifle seemed to reconsider making a move, and then suddenly jerked up the Henry and began levering it to shoot. I couldn't have cared less about which man fell, but I was curious as to how the face-off would end. Never did I expect what happened next.

Royce Dunbar drew his Colt Peacemaker, fired, and dropped his opponent before the thin man even fired his rifle. Royce then twirled the pistol and re-holstered almost before the other man hit the ground. He had actually beaten a man who was already levering a round from a repeating rifle!

I had heard of quick-draw artists who did parlor tricks such as tossing coins in the air and beating the coin drop with a fast draw. One man I knew would put a coin on the back of his right hand and then a whiskey shot glass upside down over the coin. He'd toss them both in the air, draw his pistol, shoot the glass, and then catch the coin.

This was different, however. This wasn't a harmless trick. Dunbar had drawn not only with blinding speed but had done so while facing an armed and deadly adversary. No wonder the town wouldn't challenge Thompson. Not with an enforcer like Royce Dunbar.

I stepped out into the street and looked at the body. Stepping over it, I turned and shrugged. "Not bad. Don't mind me, I'm just on my way to the hardware store."

Royce sneered as others came running to see what had happened. "Not bad my ass!"

While the others were dragging the body away, I went directly to the hardware store. Another man was just leaving as I went in. Flip was behind the counter.

"Problem out there?" he asked.

"Not any more."

Flip nodded slowly. "Can I help you with anything?"

"Sure, I need a couple of shirts and trousers for the trail. Four sets should do fine."

He pointed to a shelf across the room. "Help yourself. Anything else?"

I thought a moment. "This hat's getting a mite ratty. Maybe a new sombrero. Oh, and a couple of those wool pullovers for when it gets colder. You know, those little round caps that pull over your head and down over the ears."

"I think I can find some if you've got the cash. You going away?"

I nodded. "Yeah, but I'll be back. Thompson will probably want to talk to you about it. Got a pencil and paper?"

"Sure," he replied, retrieving them from under the counter.

"I'm gonna make a list of some sundries I want you to pack up for me. Thompson's going to explain in more detail, but I'll be needing the Conestoga for a while. Just put everything on the list in the wagon." Apparently the mere mention of Hank Thompson seemed sufficient to avoid any further questions. "Oh, and I'll be needing a shovel now."

Flip looked around and found what he was looking for.

"Gonna use it later on the trip."

The storekeeper just shrugged and brought one up from the back of the store.

"One last thing."

"And that might be?" Flip asked politely enough.

"What I'm going after is buried in a large cave and I'll be needing the barrel of black powder that I saw last time I was here. Oh, and some primer cord for it. Just leave it propped outside behind the back door, and when I leave, I'll put it in the wagon myself. Make sure I get everything on the list. Gonna be a long haul."

"No problem. Sure you don't need a water barrel?"

"Nope. Too big and bulky. Got enough weight coming back as it is. The canteens I bought should do just fine," I replied.

"Going after buried pirate treasure?" he joked.

"Oh, pirates are surely involved as far as I'm concerned, but it's not Spanish doubloons I'm after. Like I said, Hank will explain it to you. You and Curly should go look him up after we're done here."

"When are you planning on leaving?"

"Tomorrow might work. Planning to leave in the early morning so as not to ride the pass at night."

"If Hank Thompson says it's all right with him, I'll have the wagon loaded and ready by late this afternoon."

I took a roll of bills out and paid him. "If there is anything still owed, Hank and I will settle up with you when I return."

"Looks like this'll do just fine," the storekeeper replied as he pocketed the money. "As long as we get the wagon back later."

I left the shop, planning to return to my tent. I needed some privacy to reflect and rest. As I was adjusting my hat to avoid the sun's glare, I noticed three men who seemed to be staring my way from across the road. With the sun in my eyes I couldn't get a clear view of them but I did notice that one of the men had his arm in a sling. Another spit a wad of tobacco off into the dirt.

They seemed to be focusing on me specifically but at the time I just thought it was my imagination. After a while in a place like this you begin to feel like everyone is watching you. The group broke apart and the men all walked away. Since none of the men in that particular group had pointed at me, made any threatening gestures, or even moved toward me, I thought nothing more about them.

When I stretched out on the cot back in my tent, I remembered the old saying that a man's strengths are also his weaknesses. Thompson had set up an outlaw town that insured his safety but at the same time it would provide me the cover I needed to help get the women out.

After all, with the possible exception of the tent where the women were being kept prisoner, there shouldn't be any roving sentries or guards at night. Why would there be in a town where there was no law to keep? That same sense of false security could work to my advantage if I planned things right.

I didn't know if any of the women could drive a wagon team, so I had to form two separate strategies. In one I would drive the wagon, and in the other I would roam around on my horse. I fully expected to be pursued so I had to take that into consideration as well. I would need to deal with any guards found around the women's tent and finally I had to get the timing right. That would be crucial. I needed enough time to carry out my plan, and, above all, I had to be finished before everyone else in town was awake and wandering about.

I calculated it would take about five hours to finish all my preparations. That meant starting just after it turned dark and being finished and prepared to leave town well before dawn. There wasn't much else I could do at the moment, so I pulled my hat over my eyes and took a long *siesta*. In the Army you learned to grab some sleep anytime the opportunity presented itself. If I was to be up all night, I would need all the rest I could get.

Chapter Twenty-Five

One trick I had learned in the Army was to think about and repeat a specific time over and over to myself before falling asleep. I don't know if it works for others, but if I go to sleep while thinking say, 8:00 in the morning, I'll wake up at that precise time. I don't know if it is some sort of internal clock, but it works. Since I didn't want to risk sleeping through the night, I kept repeating the same time over and over. Once again it worked for me, and when I suddenly came awake, my pocket watch confirmed the time for me. It was finally dark enough for me to get started.

I got up, cleared out my possessions from the tent, and started for the livery stable. Just as I'd hoped, nobody was around, so I quickly saddled my horse and packed up the mule. Then as quietly as I could, I walked them out of the barn, mounted the Appaloosa, and rode out behind all the buildings. I went first to the hardware store where, just as I'd hoped, the Conestoga was hitched up to a team of two big draft horses and loaded with all the supplies I'd ordered.

I tied the mule to the back of the wagon, and then secured all the extra canteens I'd ordered to the back of my saddle. I put the loop of primer, or detonation cord, over the saddle horn where the lariat would have normally gone, and then removed the blasting caps I'd requested from the wagon. I checked them and made sure they were all safely padded. Then I carefully put them in my saddlebags next to the sticks of TNT I'd found back at that miner's shack. I next took a kerosene lamp out from among the supplies and hung it, too, from my saddle.

Finally I picked up that small barrel of black powder and remounted the horse. I rode out of town as quietly as I could, but, although I knew nobody would really notice any small sounds I made, the clinking of those canteens and the lamp against the saddle sounded like a brass band to me.

I had a specific destination in mind, one that I had noticed on the way into Broken Willow. There was a slight narrowing in the roadway that led into town. It was far enough from town to avoid suspicion of any sort and far enough from the pass so as not to be seen by any sentries that might be hidden up in the rocks.

After about fifteen minutes of riding, I reached the precise spot I had in mind. I dismounted, ground-tied the Appaloosa, and began my preparations by pouring the black powder from the barrel into the canteens.

It took about an hour to finish the job, and when I was done, I rode on ahead toward the pass. I had to get by the sentry but it was about 1:00 a.m. and thankfully there wasn't a full moon out. It was pitch black, just the way I wanted it.

I had previously rubbed some black mud on my hands and face to provide cover in the dark and was dressed in a black coat and shirt. I also made sure not to wear any shiny buttons or anything else that might show up at night. Perhaps the sentry was napping, I don't know, but as I sneaked around his post in the dark, there was no challenge of any kind.

I went to the rock face, ground-tied the Appaloosa, and then climbed as high as I could.

When I was finished with the preparations that I had planned previously, I climbed back down, and then rode quickly back to town. I had used up about five hours, but so far I had gone undetected.

I got back to the Conestoga wagon and retrieved all the clothing I had ordered. I put it in a sack and tied it to the saddle. After washing my face so I wouldn't scare the girls, I then rode as close as I dared to the tent where they were being kept and tied my horse to a nearby tree.

I wanted to get out of town as fast as possible, but this part of the plan required stealth not speed. I had to make sure not to alert any guards that might be roaming around the girls' tent. I simply couldn't afford to have one yell out and awake the others. That would be the surest way to fail that I could think of.

I crawled to within a few feet of the women's tent and watched for a good twenty minutes. I could actually hear my own heart beat and it took all the patience I could muster to stay still.

At the end of my wait I was convinced there was only one man guarding the front of the tent. That was when I hesitated. I knew from prior experience I could eliminate the sentry, but the question I faced was how extreme I needed to be.

I might be able to knock him out, but that meant a greater risk of him crying out, or simply making too much noise while struggling. Some folks take a blow better than others. Also, he might recover before we were gone.

While I could always immobilize him, there was still a chance that somehow he might get loose or be discovered. He would sound the alarm on us and that would mean one more pissed-off outlaw following behind.

I had taken lives in war but this wasn't exactly the same. Or was it? I suppose it was simply a question of moral justification. Regardless, it only took me a moment to decide that the lives of those women was justification enough.

I crawled an inch at a time, trying all the while not to stare at my target. I had learned a long time ago that when you stare at someone long enough, they can sense it even if they can't see you. I guess that's where the idea of a sixth sense came from. Eyes in the back of your head. True or not, I wasn't going to risk it.

After what seemed an eternity I sprang up behind the guard and, before he could react, clamped my left hand around his head and over his mouth. Sarge had taught me not to slit a sentry's throat from outside like everyone believes you should. The throat is harder than most think and you end up sawing. Sometimes the knife sticks. It is messy and a horrible job usually is made worse. Instead, I was taught to shove the knife blade in the neck sideways right up to the hilt and then push it away from the spine, cutting outward. It is quicker and quieter and more effective. That's just what I did to that sentry who dropped without a sound.

I quickly cleaned the blade on his coat and sheathed it. I retrieved the bag of clothes from the saddle and returned to the tent. When I lifted the flap, I came face to face with the girl I believed to be the colonel's niece. She gasped and put her hand to her mouth. Even in the dark under very difficult circumstances I couldn't help but to marvel at how pretty she was. Tall and brunette with big brown eyes, she was a remarkable vision. I shook my head and recovered my sense of purpose.

"Miss Grierson?" I whispered. "I'm here to rescue you."

She nodded and helped me through the tent. As I looked around, I noticed Eileen and Suzanne huddled at the back. Puzzled, I asked: "There were supposed to be four of you."

It was Eileen who responded. "Helen was the youngest and prettiest of us. As soon as we got here, that brute they call Royce took her away . . . and . . . used her. Badly." She started sobbing.

Suzanne quickly finished the explanation. "The thought that it would continue apparently was too much for her, and the next morning we found her dead. She had used a piece of broken glass to slit her wrists. There was nothing we could do. After that, Hank Thompson gave orders to the men . . . and they haven't touched the rest of us yet in that way . . . so far. . . ." She looked like she was on the verge of breaking down as well.

"There's no time for crying now. We have got to get you out of here *pronto*. Put on these clothes. I don't care how well they fit, just get into them. Use the hat and caps and pull them down low over your hair and face. You have got to pass for men." They all nodded, indicating that they understood.

I looked out the tent. "Sorry about this, but I have to hide the sentry. If anyone sees him, we're finished." I dragged the body inside the tent, rolled him under the cot, and covered it with a tarp. The Grierson girl actually grabbed one of his legs and helped me pull him in.

"Miss Grierson, can any of you drive a big wagon?" I asked quietly.

She nodded. "I can. Grew up around Army barracks. If it has four legs, I can ride it, and if it has wheels, I can drive it," she said proudly. I had to hand it to her. She was one courageous lady to be so determined. I suppose it ran in the family.

"And my name is Barbara."

"Jedidiah, but everyone calls me Badger. Now put those on. I'll be right outside."

As I left the tent, I literally bumped into another guard. I had falsely assumed they would not change sentries for the rest of the night. But then you know what they say about the word assume. It really means to make an ass out of you.

I must have startled the man for he took a short step backward. It was the wrong move. Whenever possible, you don't want to give the first offensive move to your opponent. It wasn't that I was that fast or strong, but Hackworth had long ago taught me that in a fight strength wasn't as important as knowledge.

I know where the body's vulnerable points are and how to take advantage of them. Since my opponent was stepping back, I rushed forward and pushed him farther backward, off-balancing his stance. With a sideways kicking sweep of my boot I smacked his front shin so hard he doubled over in pain, and, as he leaned forward, I hit him with an upward blow to the chin with my elbow.

I had learned long ago to avoid hitting someone directly in the face with an ungloved fist. A person's face is irregular and punches to it, or worse yet to the skull, often result in broken fingers or knuckles. It happens more often than most people realize. However the fat part of the forearm at the elbow is flat and hard as a rock. With an elbow blow nothing breaks except the other fellow's face. I heard his neck snap before he even hit the ground.

I dragged the body into the tent. I didn't know whether the girls were through changing but at this point I didn't have time for modesty. Fortunately (or unfortunately considering your point of view) the women had already donned the men's clothing and were ready to go.

I went back to the horse and retrieved a couple of knives and a pistol that I gave to the girls. They already had taken the weapons from the dead men.

"Don't shoot unless it's absolutely necessary," I warned. "Anything that makes a noise will wake everyone up and we'll be through before we even get started. Now listen up, we'll walk in twos. Barbara, you come with me. You two follow behind at a distance. Don't bunch up. If anyone spots us, I don't want it to look like we're all together. And remember, we've got to make everything look natural."

I added one more caution. "Even in the dark your . . . um . . . feminine figures might give us away, so ladies, try to lumber a little. You know, walk like a big cowboy might." Suzanne actually chuckled for a moment. I was glad I had lightened the mood although that hadn't been my intention.

"We're headed back behind the hardware store," I whispered. "I have a wagon stashed there. Now remember, quiet and steady."

I don't know why I chose Barbara to go with me except perhaps because she was Grierson's niece. Maybe it was that she seemed to be the calmest of the three. Or maybe, and I am forced to admit to the possibility, because I thought she was the prettiest of the lot.

We untied the Appaloosa and started walking leisurely back to the hardware store. Hopefully our departure appeared leisurely, but inside I was hardly relaxed. Anything out of the ordinary now would spoil everything. Another guard arriving at the tent, a night owl who couldn't sleep and decided to take a walk, or simply any unexpected noise could spell our doom.

Thankfully we made it uneventfully to the wagon. I tied the horse to the back of the Conestoga right next to the mule, and we all climbed aboard. I took the reins and indicated to Barbara to sit up front with me. I snapped the reins as quietly as I could, and the wagon started to move. I didn't stop to check my watch but it was about 4:00 or 5:00 in the morning and the town still seemed dead to the world. That was just fine with me. We were moving as quietly as possible, but I recalled an old Scottish saying. If memory serves me it goes something like: "The best laid schemes o' mice an' men gang aft agley." My personal experience was that when things "gang agley," it's always at the most inconvenient time.

Once we were free of the town limits, I put the whip to the team and we rode on as fast as we could.

After a short time Suzanne whispered from the

back of the wagon. "There are men watching at the pass."

"I know," I replied. "But they shouldn't be worrying about people leaving town. They're only interested in keeping the law out of the pass. No reason to worry about those already inside."

I hoped I sounded more convincing than I had a right to be.

"What if we're followed?" Eileen asked.

"Have to assume we will be. It won't stay this dark very long and they're bound to change the guard at your tent sooner or later. Won't take long to realize you're gone."

"So what do we do then?" Barbara asked. She was obviously very worried and with just cause. "We can't outrun men on horseback in this thing," she said knowingly.

"That's where I come in," I said, pulling the wagon to a stop.

I handed Barbara the reins and jumped down. "Just around the bend there is a guard post. About a half hour after that and you're in the pass. Give me about a five-minute head start, and then follow. If I'm not there waiting for you, then you'll have to shoot the guard with that pistol and ride like hell with your heads down."

"But . . . ," Eileen started.

"No ifs, ands, or buts. I'll be there, don't you worry. I'm just mentioning the possibility is all." I saddled up, touched the brim of my hat in an informal salute, and then rode ahead on the Appaloosa.

I hoped I'd encounter the same guard I'd met on the way in. If he recognized me, he might not be as suspicious. A wagon full of people however would surely alert him and up close he couldn't help but recognize the women even in their disguises.

It would have been a simple matter to shoot the guard from a distance with my scoped Springfield, but I was afraid we were too near to the pass. A rifle shot that close would alert the sentries up in the rocks. I needed to give that wagon as much of a chance as I could to get outside the Hole-in-the-Wall before I made any noise. I'd have to take the guard out another way.

Chapter Twenty-Six

As I rounded the bend in the trail, I slowed down very deliberately. I unsnapped the strap that held my Bowie knife in its sheath, which I wore on the left side of my belt. I spotted the outpost almost immediately. Once I got closer, I recognized the same guard who had been on duty when I first rode in.

"It's just me, remember?" I said, approaching the guard. "Time to pull out. Anything interesting happening out here I might need to worry about?"

I hadn't stopped the horse but continued slowly on while talking to him. I needed to keep him distracted.

"Oh, it's you," he said. "No, nothing going on out here. All's . . ." Before he could say "quiet," I jumped sideways off the saddle onto his back. His rifle went flying out of his hand. I pulled my Bowie knife and was about to use it when he suddenly bent over and threw me off his shoulder.

I hit the ground hard but rolled over and jumped back up onto my feet in time to see the man pull his own knife. He was a big man but thin and obviously agile. He held his knife close to his side like he knew how to use it. I hate knife fights. They're always messy and most times both adversaries end up cut to pieces.

I tried to remember in a split second everything Sergeant Hackworth had taught me about knife fighting over the years. The Army's philosophy has always been to attack the opponent's closest body part with your knife. They stick out an arm, you cut the arm. If they lean their neck in, you slice the neck. Sergeant Hackworth, however, had a different theory, one that was taught to him while he was in the Far East. He called it the ABCs of a knife fight.

In this fighting style A equals airway. The first thing you do is stab or slice to an airway whether that be throat or into the rib cage. In other words, make the opponent lose the ability to breathe. In the second phase B stands for bleeding. Here you attack the body's main blood vessels such as the ones in the throat or the big arteries inside the thighs. Finally C stands for attacking the opponent's consciousness—going for a knock-out blow to silence the man. Done properly these three moves can all be accomplished in only a second or two by a well-trained knife fighter.

Some of the braves I have known from the Plains tribes had an alternative way of fighting that translates to defanging the snake. Their theory is that if the hand can't hold the knife, the knife is worthless. They hold their weapon close to the body and try to maintain their distance so as to avoid being grabbed, blocked, or knocked down.

The idea of defanging is to wait for the attacker to expose his knife so you can quickly slash his wrist, or perhaps, if your knife is big enough, to hack off his hand or forearm. Regardless of the system used, knife fighting is messy, scary, and downright dangerous.

In this kind of a fight balance is everything, and, although Sarge didn't advocate kicking high against someone holding a knife (he always said it was a good way to get your leg slashed to pieces), he taught me that a swift, low, hard kick to the ankle or shin, or a stomp to the opponent's foot with your boot heel is usually enough to stun him.

That outpost guard actually smirked at me. He

held his knife well, but his balance was way off. Maybe he thought his longer reach and height were enough of an advantage to allow him to take me on easily, but just as Sergeant Hackworth had demonstrated so impressively years ago with that young recruit when we first met, fighting isn't about strength or size. It is about knowledge, experience, and focused intensity.

I faced that guard straight on, faked an upward arm movement, and proceeded to smash his leading shin with a quick, side-swiping, low kick using the inside of my boot. It is a blow much like the kind children use to kick a rubber ball sideways. I could actually hear his shin bone break.

Anyone who's every stubbed a shin on a bedpost knows how incredibly painful it is. As the man was dropping down in agony, I shoved my Bowie knife up into his rib cage and then sliced on through. After I pulled it free, I squatted down and drove it forward to slice his inner thigh. I pulled the knife back, and finally dropped the butt of my knife down on the back of his head.

The man died immediately but from which part of my attack I didn't know. Not counting the kick, my whole attack had taken less than three seconds. It took me longer to clean the blade and to control the reflex that almost caused me to vomit. Like I said, I hate fighting with a blade.

The wagon pulled up with the women. They looked down at me as I stood next to the body.

I didn't know exactly how to react, so I simply said: "Sorry. Couldn't be helped."

Eileen, who I had taken for the more sensitive of the three, looked at me with sympathy and said: "No need on our account. We're all Army brats of one sort or another."

I couldn't help but smile back.

"So what now?" Barbara asked.

"I'm riding back toward town," I explained.

"What in heaven's name for?" Suzanne exclaimed. The fear and worry were obvious in her voice.

"They'll be coming for us for sure by now and I have to make sure they don't reach you. There's not enough time to explain everything, so you'll have to trust me. In the meantime, keep riding as fast as you can until you get to where the pass begins. From there, slow down, and then ride on nice and easy. Keep your heads down and don't let any sentries get a good look. Remember they're all on the north slope. That'll be on your left side. Don't want to let them catch on that you're females." I added quickly: "Then, when you hear a big noise, stop and wait for me. I hope I'll catch up to you before you actually enter the pass. If more than ten minutes pass after you hear that sound, then ride on through as fast as you can and keep heading back the same way they brought you in. When you get to the miner's shack, head due south and eventually you'll get to safety."

"What sound? What will it be like?" Eileen asked.

"Oh, trust me. You'll know. Now get going. Remember, if I'm not back after ten minutes from the time you've stopped, get going and ride like all the demons from hell are on your tail." *And they probably will be,* I thought to myself.

I swung up into the saddle and rode as fast as I could back to that narrow bend in the trail we had just passed. In a little under five minutes I arrived, and, as I dismounted, I drew my Springfield Trapdoor from its saddle scabbard.

I fully cocked the rifle's hammer and raised the breech up to make sure there was a cartridge in the chamber. After snapping the trapdoor cover closed, I pulled out my telescopic scope and quickly attached it. I then lay down behind a small boulder, and waited.

So far there was nothing unusual to be seen, so I slowly moved the rifle around until I found a small target off to the side about a hundred yards away. It was a discarded kerosene lantern, half buried in the dirt. I used it to sight in the rifle.

Within a few minutes a large cloud of dust blew up and I heard the expected sound of a large number of galloping horses.

As the gang started to round the bend, I looked at those in front fully expecting to find Thompson and Dunbar. I was surprised that they were nowhere to be found and that puzzled me.

Those two didn't seem to be the type to let others do their dirty work. They were the sort who took great satisfaction in extracting their own revenge. I took another look and realized that one of the riders out in front of the pack was the same man I'd noticed with the sling on his arm back in town.

Through the magnification of the scope I finally recognized him as the man who called himself Wilkins. The very same man Lobo and I had had the run-in with back in Cooper's Crossing. The one Jake Finley had run out of town. I suddenly had a sinking feeling in the pit of my stomach but I had a job to do, so I set about doing it.

I quickly calculated the time remaining, aimed my rifle at that buried lantern, and pulled the trigger. It was an easy shot. Hell, I was the one who'd rigged and buried the lantern in the first place.

To the men on horseback there appeared to be nothing unusual out ahead of them so the whole group was bunched up and riding at full tilt. When I fired my shot, the lamp immediately exploded in flames. The fire touched off the detonation cord I'd buried and the gang rode right into a series of simultaneous explosions from a combination of TNT and exploding canteens full of black powder and nails.

I ducked behind the boulder, and when the dust finally settled, there was a bloody mass of downed horses and men. I hadn't seen anything that bad since the war.

I didn't stop to count, but even a quick glance told me I had succeeded. The blast had almost totally eliminated the gang, either killing or seriously wounding nearly all the outlaws. Those who could still ride were hightailing it back to Broken Willow and would no longer pose a serious threat to us.

I ran as fast as I could over to the Appaloosa and sheathed the rifle in its scabbard. It took me a moment or so to get into the saddle as the blast had spooked the horse a little. Once I was mounted, I let out a whoop and galloped away, back toward the wagon.

As I'd directed, the girls had stopped just short of the entrance to the pass. I dismounted and quickly retied my horse to the back of the wagon. I once again drew the Springfield and then practically dived into the wagon bed from behind.

"Drive on, Barbara, but remember, nice and steady," I said. "We don't want to spook the look-outs."

I readjusted the scope and stretched out with the rifle sticking sideways, just slightly out from under the Conestoga's cover. I sighted along the rock wall where I knew the sentries would be waiting. I didn't know whether the guards had any binoculars or not, so I reminded the girls to keep their hats pulled low and not to look up.

We were halfway into the pass when several men stood up from their hiding places in the rocks and shouted down: "Hey, what in hell just happened back there?"

I didn't want them to see me and knew they would recognize a girl's voice if one of them shouted back. I whispered without taking my eyes off the rifle: "Don't answer them. Just keep on going, but don't rush it. Nice and easy. Make it look like we're not in any rush."

Barbara was driving the wagon with Susanne and Eileen in back with me. They shouted again, and Barbara raised her hands up wide at them as if she had no clue. I had to hand it to her, she had real grit.

After another shout one of the sentries ordered us to halt.

"What now?" Barbara asked without turning around.

"Keep on going just like you are until I tell you," I replied, still keeping my eyes on the rifle scope, "then let 'er rip."

At that point I heard another order to halt followed almost immediately by a shot. At the sound of a second shot I pulled the trigger on my Trapdoor. The explosion that followed was about as I had expected.

Because, last night, after laying that first row of charges at the bend, I rode even farther ahead, sneaked past the guard, and climbed the rock face to a point over the sentry stations. There I had placed the remainder of my TNT and the rest of the black powder and some of the blasting caps.

This last explosion, triggered by my rifle shot, brought down an avalanche of rocks that took out the remainder of the guards.

I rolled over and breathed a sigh of relief. "Now, Barbara, put the whip to 'em." I felt the wagon lurch forward, and we rode on at a fast pace for about ten minutes. The two women in the back hugged each other, and then both of them gave me a hug and said their thanks.

I was about as relieved and happy as I can remember being for a very long time when I suddenly heard Barbara gasp loudly and bring the wagon to a halt. I climbed forward and out onto the wagon's front seat to the right of Barbara to see what was up.

Staring right at us and blocking our way were Hank Thompson and Royce Dunbar. Barbara had been right to stop. At that close a range if she had tried to gallop the wagon over them, she would surely have been shot right out of her seat.

When the wagon came to a stop, I started to climb down. As I did so, I untied the rawhide thong at the bottom of the holster that secured it to my leg. Before finally dropping to the ground, I cocked both barrels of the shotgun and whispered to Barbara: "If this doesn't go well, empty the pistol I gave you at them, and then drive as fast as you can. It may be your last chance. But not until and unless . . ." I didn't finish the sentence.

"Oh, please, be careful. These men are born killers," she pleaded.

I walked around and placed myself in front of the wagon's team, directly facing the two men. I was now positioned between them and the women in the wagon. Dunbar was facing me a little to my left and Thompson on my right, standing near him.

"It was Wilkins, wasn't it?" I asked calmly.

Royce smirked back at me. "Damn' right it was."

"Seems he recognized you from back in Cooper's Crossing. You two had a previous little run-in, I hear," Hank Thompson said angrily. "Apparently the sheriff let on you were some sort of bounty man," he added. "Trying to collect, are you?"

"Yeah, good luck with that," Royce said, and laughed.

"So I assume you two came through here earlier just in case I made it past the guards," I said. Out of habit my right hand was now resting on my scatter-gun.

"You got that right," Royce replied.

"Just curious. Why'd you let us get this far? Why not just stop us back in town?" I asked.

Hank was the first to answer. "Was a good test

of our defenses. It let me know who I could depend on."

I just nodded. "Well, your gang did go down on your behalf. I'll give them that."

"I gather those explosions were your doing and that our men won't be following?" Thompson added.

I looked at Royce Dunbar. "You got that right," I mimicked. "So it's just the three of us now." I sounded confident, but truthfully I had seen Dunbar draw and I assumed Hank Thompson was just as fast. With his pistols positioned as they were with their butts forward, I assumed he used what they call a twist draw.

"Two to one suits me just fine," Royce added happily.

"Thought it might," I stated dryly.

"Before we kill you, though, I'd like to know why you would take on such odds all by your lonesome for women who are complete strangers to you. You need money that bad?"

"Oh, I wanted to help those girls all right, but I didn't come just for them. I really came for you," I explained.

Not surprisingly they both looked a little puzzled.

"Us? I didn't think any lawman even knew we were here," Hank said seriously.

"Yeah. Last I heard there ain't even posters out on us," Royce said.

"There aren't," I said. "Least not under those names,"

"So why us? Before we kill you, I'd like to know," Hank said.

"Personal reasons," I said after a pause.

"And those might be?" he asked. "I don't recall your face."

"Let me help," I replied. "Took me a long time to find you, but now I understand why. You changed your names and cleaned up your act. Stayed here instead of going back out on the trail." I addressed Thompson directly. "You used to go by Clay rather than Hank, right?"

Henry Clayton Thompson. He looked at Royce Dunbar, and then back at me. He tipped his hat up slightly as if to study me further. "Used to. Some who're close to me still call me that from time to time."

"Then you'll be the first to go, Clay. I've waited a long time for this," I said, glancing over at Royce. "That is unless you two are so cowardly you have to try me together."

"That'll be the day," Dunbar growled. "Let me take him, Hank," he said angrily.

Thompson shook his head. "Nope. I've got this. Personal, hey? Waited a long time, huh? Mind telling me for what?"

"For a village full of innocent Arapahoes." I replied. I was so mad the words almost stuck in my throat.

"Whoa, that was a long time ago. You've been looking for us since 'way back then?" He shook his head from side to side. "How sad. All that time searching for us just to end up dead. What a shame," he said, gloating. "Well, we might as well get this done."

I considered my chances, which at the time were poor to slim. My rifle was still in the back of the wagon and I only carried two rounds in my sidearm. And both of these two were faster on the draw than a lightning strike. Suddenly I knew how all this would play out. I took a big, slow breath and let out a sigh of relief. Thompson and I were tensed and squared away, facing each other. In the corner of my eye I also watched Royce. I was fairly sure that between Thompson's order and Royce's confidence in his partner, Royce would hold his fire. Even so, I didn't want to take any chances by ignoring him.

"If you know what's good for you, Thompson, I'd advise you to turn around and look behind you," I warned suddenly.

Henry Clay Thompson laughed out loud. "That's the best you got? You actually think I've lived all these years by falling for that old one?"

"OK, then," I said, "but before we go at it, let me ask you just one more thing. Ever seen what a timber wolf can do to a man?"

"No, and what of it?" he asked puzzled. "We've never had any wolves around here."

"You do now," I replied, smiling.

They say that as you are about to die your senses heighten. At least Thompson's did and he suddenly spun around.

"Lobo, gun!" I yelled. Actually the command wasn't really needed as that wolf was already in mid-air, springing right at him. To me it always seemed that Lobo could somehow sense anger, fear, or evil in people. Thompson had all three and Lobo never let up once he started in on him.

I turned to face Dunbar. Royce knew that if he turned to help his friend or tried to fire on the wolf it would give me the advantage I needed to shoot him dead. His face reflected the hate he felt for me, but I also sensed something else. Fear.

The screams coming from what was happening to his best friend of so many years had to have been unnerving. However, as sadistic as it may sound, it was music to my ears. I had never felt so alive.

I now faced only one man. Even as fair as that might sound, the enemy in front me was as deadly with a handgun as anyone I'd ever seen, and his fast draw holster held a six-shot Colt Peacemaker.

Out the corner of his eye Royce Dunbar quickly glanced over at his partner. He rubbed his chin with his left hand as if in thought. His right was resting on the butt of his Colt. "I know who you are now," he said.

"You do, huh?" I replied.

"Bounty hunter who travels with a wolf-dog mutt," he said. "You gotta be the one they call the Badger."

"Some call me that."

"So why were we so almighty important to you? Personal, you said? And how'd you finally find out we was here? You say it took you all these years to track us down, but you ain't no lousy Injun. What I wanna know is, what's so god-damned important to you about a few savages being killed all them years ago."

"Still don't recognize me, do ya?"

He looked at me with his half-cocked head and squinted. "Should I?"

"I'll answer your questions in order. Then you can try to kill me."

"Oh, trust me, I'll do more than try," he snarled.

"You used to wear a big beard." I said it more as a statement than a question. "And they used to call you Brick."

Dunbar looked a little surprised. "He used to," he said referring to Clay Thompson. "Always said I was built like one."

"Or maybe he just thought your head was as thick as one," I offered.

"Screw you, bounty man," he rasped angrily.

"Well, Brick, you asked me a question, so I'll tell you. When I heard about that train robbery, I interviewed all the witnesses I could find. They described you pretty damned well and said that the shooting didn't start until one of the passengers started to argue. Apparently he ripped off your bandanna in the scuffle that occurred between you two."

"So? What's that got to do with anything?"

I knew he'd want his curiosity settled before he made his move.

"A little unusual to kill a man over a lousy scarf, isn't it? Unless, of course, there's something underneath it you wanted to hide."

The big man just glared at me.

"Take it off, Brick," I said firmly. "Take the kerchief off now so I can see the scar. That's why your head is stuck sideways like that, isn't it? Scarred down."

Royce Dunbar pulled off the bandanna, revealing as ugly a mess of scar tissue as I'd ever seen. It only served to intensify the anger and hate in his eyes.

"I'll bet it hurt like hell at the time," I said. "You sure must want to get even with the one who gave you that."

"Oh, I already did just that."

"Did ya now?" I asked. I then reached up with my left hand and pulled something out of my shirt pocket. My right hand, like Brick's, was resting on the butt of my scatter-gun. I threw him the object I'd retrieved from my pocket. He caught it with his left and with surprising dexterity.

He never once looked away or moved his right arm.

"Her hair was red," I said with a building fury. "Just like mine."

He glanced quickly down at the woman's silver broach in his hand and at once realized who I was and why I was there.

"You survived? After all this time? All this . . . ? It had nothing to do with the women, after all?"

"Oh, it had everything to do with the women. Especially the one who was my mother, you cowardly raping son-of-a-bitch."

I was close enough, even with my poor eyesight, to see Brick Dunbar's eyelids twitch just once before he went for his gun.

When someone truly knows what they are doing, I swear there is nothing on God's green earth as fast on the draw as a Colt Peacemaker pulled from the kind of holster Brick Dunbar wore. And Dunbar clearly knew what he was doing. Nothing, but nothing is as fast on the draw as a Colt from a rig like that. Nothing that is, except a weapon that doesn't even need to be drawn.

When I had gone to that leather smith back in Cooper's Crossing, Mr. Murphy had not only repaired my belt and holster, but he had also made one very important modification, just as I'd requested. What he'd done was to add a small brass bolt that connected the holster to a grooved metal slide attached to the belt. In essence Murphy had created a holster swivel.

I no longer had to draw. By first undoing the tie-down thong from off my leg that holster now hung free. I'd also made sure when I climbed down off the wagon that both hammers of my shotgun were already cocked. When Brick Dunbar finally went for his pistol, I simply pushed down on the sawed-off scatter-gun's stock. That move swiveled the front of the holster upward when I pulled the trigger.

Brick took both shotgun barrels waist high, horizontally and right through the open bottom of my holster.

After that there wasn't much of him left to bury. I went over and retrieved my mother's broach from his death grip. I cleaned it off and replaced it in my pocket.

"Let's go back, Lobo," I said softly. He looked up at me from what now remained of Clay Thompson's body and I swear he seemed to be smiling. I walked back around the wagon with Lobo trotting behind me. I checked on the horse and mule, and once I was confident they were both still secured, I walked around to the front of the Conestoga and climbed up. I looked over at Barbara and the other two girls. They seemed to be stunned into silence.

"The quicker we leave here, the better off we'll be," I pointed out, taking the reins from Barbara's hands. "Time to get you three back to the fort. I expect there are some overly anxious folks there that'll be mighty happy to see you."

"Wish Helen were coming with us," Elaine said sadly.

"I do, too," I said. "Sorry I couldn't have gotten here sooner. Did my best to try."

"You did more than your best," Barbara said, putting her hand on my arm. She leaned over and kissed me on the cheek. I looked over at her into those beautiful eyes but all I could do to express my thanks was nod.

Epilogue

After two days of riding we crossed paths with a cavalry patrol from the fort. They appeared to be armed to the teeth and as could have been predicted the ever impatient Captain Boyle was leading the troop. But don't get me wrong, at the time I was more than happy to have their company.

After an emotional reunion with his fiancée, Suzanne, and a rather uncomfortable explanation of why we were one short, I turned to the captain. "So whatever happened to all that Posse Comitatus crap?" I asked.

"Nothing in it says we can't perform a routine patrol in our area of responsibility," the captain replied, grinning sheepishly. He never took his arm from around Suzanne's waist for a moment.

"Mister Kershaw, I am sorry for how I behaved toward you earlier. I am eternally in your debt."

"No need to be. But thanks anyway. And call me Badger. Everyone else does."

Captain Boyle finally ordered the troop to remount and assigned a driver for the wagon. After all we'd been through I half expected Barbara to insist on driving it herself but she seemed fine just riding along as a passenger with her two friends. I remounted the Appaloosa and we all headed off, back to Fort Russell.

Over the next few days I spent as much time as I could with Barbara, and the more time I spent near her the more relaxed I felt whenever she was around. I was ill at ease whenever I stopped to think of all the horrendous acts she had seen me commit, but if any of it bothered her, she gave no indication of any animosity toward me.

Barbara was a warm and caring person to just about everyone she met, but I grew to hope that her emotional responses to me weren't merely attempts to be courteous or kind-hearted. Maybe I had no right to get my hopes up, but I wanted it to be more than that.

At night the troopers tended to allow the women their privacy. All except Captain Boyle, that is, who seemed to spend most of the time escorting his fiancée around. I certainly couldn't fault him for that since I couldn't help checking in on Barbara more than was really necessary.

If my actions were too forward, or if they were as obvious as I expect they were to everyone else, she gave no indications of wanting me to back off. Quite the contrary, we began to spend our evenings around the campfire, swapping stories. Truthfully I have to admit that I tended to swap more than she did. Barbara listened much more attentively than I was ever capable of.

Actually the ride back to the fort from that point on was a rather an unremarkable journey, but it did give me a sense of pride and well-being to be riding once again with the U.S. cavalry troopers I respected so much.

On account of the women we didn't rush the trip and so it took us several days longer than usual to finally reach Fort D.A. Russell. About as expected, everyone there was in great spirits. Everyone, that is, except Helen's relatives. I left the explanations about what had happened to her to the other women. As I've said, I was never comfortable with that sort of thing.

The major, as befitting his command, immediately offered me a commission as scout if I would reënlist, but there was no way I was getting sucked back into that life. I made plans to leave for home, but strangely I now began to experience a sort of emptiness. I had spent almost my entire life seeking an end to my pain and now that it was all over, I somehow felt a bit lost.

I'd be going back to my valley, that much I knew for sure. Lord knows there was still a lot to do there and I'd be kept busy enough, but, even with Sarge as company, for the first time that ranch seemed a lonely destination.

After a day in the fort and all the back thumping I could handle, I made preparations to ride out. The last thing I did before leaving was to seek out Barbara Grierson. I walked her over to a quiet corner of the yard and reached into my pocket. "I'd like you to have this," I said, handing over the silver broach. "It belonged to my mother. She was a very special person."

Barbara looked down at the broach. "I know you've carried this a long time and how much it means to you." She thought for a moment. "Thank you. I'm touched you'd think of me. I'd be honored to have it." She looked up into my eyes and for a moment I didn't know what to say. There have been times in my life when I have wanted to find the right words, to say certain things, but my emotions got the better of me. This was one of those awkward moments.

Barbara smiled back at me and sensed my embarrassment. Changing the subject, she asked: "So, tell me, and truthfully now. Why does every-one call you Badger?"

I looked into her eyes and laughed. "I was raised

by the Arapaho Indians. When I was child, my mother had gone to their tribe as a missionary. The Indians didn't have a translation in their language for Jedidiah Kershaw so they nicknamed me Little Badger. I don't think there was a special reason for it. The chief just liked how it fit me, I guess. Who knows, maybe he saw a badger the day he decided to name me?

"Anyway, our camp was raided by Thompson's men when the braves were away. After my ma was killed, the rest of the tribe returned and found me half dead with my skull practically stove in. They nursed me back to health and sort of adopted me. I grew up among them and the nickname stuck. I had gotten used to it, so after I left I kept using the English translation. Thus the Badger. Got rid of the Little part pretty quickly, though."

Barbara laughed. "I can see why."

We walked together over to my horse. I tied our ever-present companion, the jack mule, to the Appaloosa's saddle, and then untied the horse from the hitching post.

Barbara looked concerned. "I am going to see you again, aren't I?" she asked as I mounted up.

"You can count on it," I replied. I suddenly felt much better and actually began to recover a sense of purpose. "Trust me, I'll be back very soon." I leaned down from the horse and gave her a kiss. "In the meantime, give some thought to ranch life." Her smile gave me all the answer I needed.

I sat back up in the saddle a very happy man. "Lobo, heel!" I shouted as I galloped away. The big mutt ran after me and I swear we were both grinning the whole time.

About the Author

R. W. Stone inherited his love for Western adventure from his father, a former Army Air Corps armaments officer and horse enthusiast. He taught his son both to ride and shoot at a very early age. Many of those who grew up in the late 1950s and early 1960s remember it as a time before urban sprawl when Western adventure predominated both television and the cinema, and Stone began writing later in life in an attempt to recapture some of that past spirit he had enjoyed as a youth. In 1974 Stone graduated from the University of Illinois with honors in Animal Science. After living in Mexico for five years, he later graduated from the National Autonomous University's College of Veterinary Medicine and moved to Florida. Over the years he has served as President of the South Florida Veterinary Medical Association, the Lake County Veterinary Medical Association, and as executive secretary for three national veterinary organizations. Dr. Stone is currently the Chief of Staff of the Veterinary Trauma Center of Groveland, an advanced level care facility. He is the author of over seventy scientific articles and has lectured internationally. Still a firearms collector, horse enthusiast, and now a black-belt-ranked martial artist, R. W. Stone presently lives in Central Florida with his wife, two daughters, one horse, and three dogs.

Center Point Large Print
600 Brooks Road / PO Box 1
Thorndike, ME 04986-0001 USA

(207) 568-3717

US & Canada:
1 800 929-9108
www.centerpointlargeprint.com